EAGLES NEAR THE CARCASE

EAGLES NEAR THE CARCASE

by

PETER SOMERVILLE-LARGE

LONDON
VICTOR GOLLANCZ LTD
1977

© Peter Somerville-Large 1977

ISBN 0 575 02246 9

ACKNOWLEDGEMENT

I am grateful to Messrs Martin Secker and Warburg Limited for permission to quote from *My Mother's House* by Colette, translated by Una Vincenzo Troubridge.

P.S.-L.

MADE AND PRINTED IN GREAT BRITAIN BY
THE GARDEN CITY PRESS LIMITED
LETCHWORTH, HERTFORDSHIRE
SG6 1JS

For wheresoever the carcase is, there will the
eagles be gathered together.

St Matthew xxiv:28

Chapter one

A WHIFF OF cirrus horsetails straddling the blue Sevillian sky was followed by banks of cloud that appeared out of nowhere. There were a few light showers lasting ten minutes at the most. Men who perspired under the cruel sun looked up from their work with a new hope that the dry belt that extended from Senegal to Southern Spain might be broken. The monotonous daily forecast: *"buen tiempo, pocas nubes o despejado"* could change at last. In Seville they might modify the system of water rationing. In the countryside the Virgins who had been taken out of their shrines and paraded round the parched fields could go home again for a well-earned rest before their Easter exertions. They hadn't done badly. The drought had not destroyed the great southern harvests. In the Jerez vineyards drivers perched above glittering heaps of grapes, their faces pepper and salt with sweat and stubble. They scratched their dirty singlets and tucked them into their patched corduroy trousers as they yelled at their animals to move loads over chalk-coloured tracks to vats and cellars. From early sunrise families picked cotton. Along the newly reclaimed land on the banks of the Guadalquivir the rice harvest, regulated by river water, was in full swing. Giant combines spewing straw rumbled across the skyline frightening the geese newly arrived from all over northern and central Europe. Skeins dipped and rose above the desiccated marshes, their mournful honking crying out for rain.

On the Coto Doñana there was none of the activity of harvest. The *marismas* dried up and turned to hard stretches of desert, empty except for the odd vulture-picked skeleton of a deer or a bullock. The birds that died also left skeletons; but these seemed to crumble and mix with the powdery surface of the wilderness. Nothing flourished except vipers.

Those first showers proved illusory, resulting in nothing but sweeping skies and burning sunsets. The hot rainless weather returned. Few of the scientists at the *Estación Biologica* could remember such a cruel autumn. Some of us wondered if the shift

7

in world climate that had brought famine to north Africa would permanently affect the wild life of Doñana. During the last few years man had sought to destroy the quivering life on the marshes and on the sand flats by more efficient means than merely shooting it or sticking it with spears. Draining marshes and turning them into rice fields quickly upset the ecological balance. Villas and holiday houses along the last stretches of wild sea shore in south-western Spain made unfriendly boundaries. And now drought was helping to kill off the birds.

It is interesting to speculate how many times life on this great swamp had been threatened by drought. Features of the landscape never remained static for long; weather and the course of the Guadalquivir constantly changed the locations of sand, scrub and water. The Coto Doñana proper consists of about sixty-seven thousand acres and there are similar stretches of wilderness to the north and south of it. It was originally formed by silt washed down by the river. Its modern shape is startlingly recent by geological standards if one remembers that in Roman times it was dominated by the vanished lake of Lagustinus. During the middle ages, when the Dukes of Medina Sidonia took it over as their hunting preserve, they must have experienced many long dry seasons when there were fewer pigs to spear and bustards to fall to their blunderbusses. But now it seemed possible that nature had waited until the place became a sanctuary before completing the process of slaughter begun by huntsmen. Would a capricious change in trade winds ironically destroy the environment which had only just been saved from devastation caused by greed?

Doñana has always been remarkable for birds. Sandwiched between Europe and Africa it is an important staging post on the migratory routes of a bewildering number of different birds travelling north and south. The region offers them marsh, scrub, savannah, stone-pine forest, lakes and salt marshes, and attracts something like three hundred different species. Some breed here, others come and go seasonally. In addition animals flourish—wild boar, some of the last in Europe, several species of deer and the European lynx which is extinct elsewhere.

Around ten years ago the ornithologist world suddenly learned that the area was threatened by business interests which proposed buying most of it and turning it into *arrozals*—rice beds. A cam-

8

paign was hurriedly initiated to preserve "the Gibraltar of birds" for future generations. The old hunting estate of the Dukes of Medina Sidonia was purchased with the aid of the World Wild Life Fund; the Spanish government cooperated in establishing the *Estacion Biologica* and turning the old Ducal palace into a headquarters for international scientific study.

The palace is more like an overgrown farmhouse. The white-washed building was constructed out of ballast stones from ships that travelled to England with sherry and returned without a cargo. In the old days hunting parties, peppered with royal personages, were accommodated here; now it houses scientists of every nationality who choose to come and study birds, mammals, reptiles, insects and flora round and about. Tourists can stay as well, if they are willing to pay; the palace is as expensive as the most expensive *parador* without the comfort. But no *parador* can offer the chance of seeing flamingoes, spoonbills, great bustards, imperial eagles and lynxes. Hunters are also welcomed; of course they are not allowed to shoot on the *Estación* proper, but the area outside its boundaries is still available to sportsmen and the palace provides a convenient headquarters.

I came to the *Estación Biologica* for a rest from scientific and writing activities. It was not my first visit, but this time I planned to stay for a long time—perhaps as much as six months. As usual the palace was filled with ornithologists. I found them a difficult lot. The rescue of Doñana from rice exploiters was a miracle of international cooperation, but the worthy efforts of princes and dukes and duck artists had results that were not anticipated. Sometimes as I sat in the palace drawing room, which was as large as a swimming pool, and listened to Patterson's lectures on the greeting calls of storks or the painfully familiar courting routine of great crested grebes, I reflected that a permanent refuge had been created, not only for the birds, but for bores. Lindstrom and Patterson were prime examples.

Most of us were short tempered that autumn. After all, we were supposed to be conservationists, part of a sad group. Conservationists spend their lives like generals after defeats in battle, receiving endless dispatches about disaster. When the crowds alter the green places out of recognition and sprinkle them with garbage, we are the first to learn about it. In addition the drought worried us. Several people talked about abandoning their pet projects

9

and preparing estimates of bird mortality. Others twittered about their grants because the lack of rain held up their work. Late in October their worries slackened when the clouds began to gather again. But the weather still hesitated to change and the thundery atmosphere continued to make us irritable, in spite of the likelihood of rain.

The evening that Patterson began to quarrel with me I was in a particularly tetchy mood. I had let myself run out of provisions. Each guest at the palace was supposed to provide his own food supply. This ensured that the staff had to cook a couple of dozen different menus daily, according to the ingredients supplied. Nothing could have been devised to create more work. And yet the women down in the kitchen managed to be constantly cheerful, in contrast to the people they cooked for. There was an old cook whose white hair looked as if she had arranged it with an egg beater; two pretty daughters and some girls in from the surrounding countryside also maintained a constant good humour that extended beyond mealtimes. During most of the day they could be heard singing snatches of Flamenco, their voices rivalling those of any bird outside. They bustled around with the cheerful resignation of Spanish women who know that never, never, will any man attempt to relieve them of household drudgery.

When I entered the kitchen to ask if eggs or something better were available, the girls smiled and giggled as Pablo, the haughty butler, told me that I might be served a slender *tortilla con jamón* together with chicken noodle soup. Chicken noodle soup out of a packet has become a modern Spanish standby; in any inn in the High Pyrenees Miranda would be served with the muck. Perhaps, Pablo grinned, knowing with whom I was on bad terms, I might ask some of the other guests to share their menu. Señor Goncourt had obtained a chunk of *merluza* which he required to be served *a la madrileña* with a garnish of mushrooms. *Merluza*, I knew, was hake, and the thought of cadging some off old Goncourt did not stir my taste buds. Señor Patterson was sharing a chicken with Señor Smith; even now Maria was preparing it in a bed of rice. It smelled good. So did the score of other dishes, each different, bubbling and simmering for less improvident guests.

I stumped upstairs where the crew of a Spanish television team was groping its way to the dining room. Since the oil crisis the generator was only started when the last fragment of sunlight was sucked out of deepening shadows. The team was agitated. In the dusk their excited conversation, peppered with curses and the word *espaduladas*, sounded as if it referred to culinary or artistic frustrations; in fact, uninformed slobs, they were lamenting that they had arrived at the wrong time of the year to film spoonbills. Their employer took no notice of their grievances, but ignored them completely. He strode through the dining room where Pablo was at last turning on the kerosene lamps, to join a party of jovial huntsmen who were preparing to feast separately on some dish involving truffles and cream. The camera crew settled down at the same long table as the scientists to a humbler menu. Outside the long windows there was the bark of deer, a last skein of geese wheeled around the small artificial lake beside the palace, and in an overworked scenario the watery golden ball of the sun dipped beneath the horizon.

The scientists were a mixed crowd. There was Miguel, in appearance a Spanish Lytton Strachey, tall and emaciated, whose field of study was the azure-winged magpie. Juan Espinar, now drinking gazpacho, was doing research on the mongoose for his B.Sc. Unkind colleagues had suggested that he obtained most of his information from watching the antics of Josefina, the pet palace mongoose. Bossy Dr Horez behaved as if he had some sort of official status at the *Estación Biologica*; he was a local man from one of the sherry towns, which perhaps gave him a pro-prietary feeling about Doñana. His meal was milk-dominated because of his ulcer. There were two Frenchmen at the table; Goncourt, now wolfing his *merluza*, claimed relationship with the brothers and was keen on discovering a new species of pondweed for the glory of France. Hubert, sharing Juan Espinar's gazpacho, had been seconded to Doñana from his work in the Camargue, where he was a government-appointed naturalist. An Argentinian, Luiz Carnera, was a hepatologist; in his small room off the laboratory were innumerable bottled snakes. Two resident ringers and two girl botanists, all from the University of Malaga, sat together at the end of the table. One girl was pretty, one dark and moustached, both, nearly every male in the place concluded, were chaste.

Opposite me sat Heller and Lindstrom attacking an elaborate concoction of stuffed tomatoes and braised veal. Their stiff appearance was due partly to the fact that they were saddle-sore after riding all day, and partly because they were so formally dressed. Nearly everyone at the table had changed for the evening meal. The contingent from the British Isles was the exception. I never wasted time changing after getting up from my type-writer. But I hardly dressed as casually as Smith and Patterson. Smith's khaki clothes smelt, and Patterson's grey sweater and faded jeans were almost as filthy. He spent a lot of time cutting up the tibia attached to his half chicken, as if he were dissecting something more interesting than a drumstick. At the same time he directed in his loud Glaswegian accent the conversation in three languages that was being conducted around approximately one-third of the long table.

As usual the topic was gloomy and as usual it concerned the Guadalquivir delta. Most of us believed in our hearts that the demands of ricegrowers and tourists would inevitably destroy this wild part of Andalusia. In due course the reserve would become little more than a park in the middle of paddy fields and tourist towns. Would eagles and African vultures continue to soar over the new eighteen-hole golf courses? We were all pessimistic, believing that destruction could not be avoided, merely the pace of destruction decelerated. Lindstrom had recently been to a conference in Madrid on the future of the reserve. The minister in attendance had expressed indifference to such questions as whether the survival of rarities like the elusive purple herons should be allowed to compete with the demands of tourism.

"I told him that it would only cost the price of an aeroplane to buy enough land to keep the Coto safe for all time. What do you think he said? Tourists are more interested in seeing animals. Deer and wild boar. For most people watching birds is too strenuous a pastime. This was the result of a small survey of visitors to this very palace."

There was a suggestion from one of the Frenchmen that that particular minister might lose his job in one of the periodical political reshuffles following Franco's death. Possibly with changes of government there might be new attitudes towards conservation ... though of course the face of the Quadalquivir delta would have low priority during any period of political turmoil. On the other hand, someone remarked, political chaos might mean that agricultural or tourist development in the area would be deferred indefinitely.

"What you are suggesting," Patterson said, "is that the Coto Doñana needs another civil war to preserve it." He repeated the remark in his awful Spanish. The silence that followed was broken by a guffaw from the separate table.

Tourists were endured, but huntsmen were usually resented by the scientific community. This group feasting so lavishly struck us as particularly offensive. Perhaps because of its wealth— emphasized by aggressively well-cut sports clothes and expensive hunting gear about which its members shouted boasts of costs and performance. Perhaps because they chose to come and kill at a time of drought—when anything that fell to their guns would be half-starved. Also they pointedly regarded us as their inferiors.

"*Madrileños*," muttered Hubert, who always hated visitors to the palace, which he tended to regard as something like his own property.

"Not all of them," I said. "The Maharajah is entertaining again."

"Ah!" Hubert tilted back his chair so that he could glimpse the fat man who was directing the opening of champagne bottles and at the same time, if we judged correctly by his gestures and the sniggers and laughter of his guests, telling improper stories. The Maharajah was a frequent visitor to the palace, usually bringing with him a group of noisy guests. We wasted a lot of time hating him. He was dressed eccentrically in old-fashioned jodhpurs, the kind that stuck out on either side of the hip, giving his plump torso the appearance of a two-handled jug. Together with his bullying manner, they had earned him his nickname, which had been taken up by the palace staff, even by Pablo. Not by Horez, however, who was now hissing at Hubert to talk more quietly.

"Don Sanchez brings distinction to the *Estación Biologica* when he chooses to entertain here. Also his parties provide us with much needed income . . ."

Hubert said, "We all know that tomorrow they are going hunting. It is a betrayal of the function of the *Estación*. How can it measure up with concepts of conservation?"

"Naturally they will go outside the reserve. And they will not touch the protected species."

"In which case," I said, "there's very little that they can shoot legally." Recently the Spanish government had introduced a few

13

belated conservation measures like prohibiting the slaughter of birds of prey, spoonbills, black storks, white storks, marbled teal and white-headed duck. And locally a ministerial order had banned the hunting of all species of water-birds throughout the south-west provinces of Seville, Cadiz and Huelva.

Hubert said, "It will mean another massacre of partridges. Not to mention all the mammals Don Sanchez and his friends are at liberty to kill."

Patterson said, "They are only here for the deer." Smith gave a guffaw.

Dr Horez insisted, "Don Sanchez is an experienced and con-scientious hunter. You know yourself that well planned and selective hunting programmes must encourage conservation programmes."

Hubert shrugged his shoulders. "There are too many con-scientious hunters in Spain."

Miguel agreed. "You will never change the habits of Spaniards. Rich and poor, they have been brought up to hunt. It is the manly sport. How can the wild life of Spain be preserved when every small town has its shop for *cazar* crammed with elaborate hunting equipment?"

"It is a matter of re-education," old Goncourt said patronizingly.

I could not resist a dig at his own country. "But in France attitudes towards hunting are scarcely different. They are probably even more pronounced because of gastronomic encouragement to the slaughter of wild birds."

Hubert backed me up against his countryman. "There is nothing in Europe like the new appreciation of wild nature that you find in English-speaking countries. This seems to have been brought about by careful and repeated publicity."

"Publicity has its drawbacks," Patterson put in swiftly. I groaned; he was about to start on one of his pet themes. "It can bring about disasters. It encourages vandalism. In England you need what amounts to a military guard so that the military orchid can bloom. And look what happens to ospreys."

Everyone present had heard of the perpetual siege which turns Inverness-shire into a battleground in spring.

"Egg collectors are not motivated by publicity," I objected.

"How do you know?"

"Perhaps they are helped a little by reports in the press. But it doesn't take an article in the *Daily Telegraph* to let them know when and where the birds are nesting. Illicit collecting needs instinct, enterprise and an ear for local gossip. The ospreys would be robbed whether or not the sites of their nests were publicized."

"There is no need to make egg robbers' tasks any easier," Patterson said.

"They are scum," Hubert said so loudly that heads at the jolly end table turned to look at him. Among naturalists egg collecting is the unforgivable sin—like sheep-worrying in dogs or child-molesting in humans.

Miguel pointed out that for many years the protection of Scottish ospreys had been successful. The round-the-clock vigils had meant that numerous birds could mature.

"And yet there is an irony," he murmured. "Many of the ospreys that grow up in Scotland with such painstaking aid from the ornithologists are ultimately shot by huntsmen in West Africa. The rings on their feet are happily sent back to those organizations that made all the exertions to protect them."

"Nothing will stop the decline of predators," said Lindstrom. "Recently I was at a conference in Vienna on this very subject . . ." Lindstrom was an inveterate conference-goer.

I said, "Perhaps what is needed is a few more good bird books published in Africa."

This was enough to set Patterson off again. Puffing away at his stinking Duocados, he muttered that the trouble about popularization was that it meant money going to the wrong people.

"Nowadays with recessions and cutbacks it's difficult to squeeze out any decent grants—unless one happens to be given the purse of gold from the National Geographic people."

"For that," Miguel said, "you have to be oh so persuasive and garrulous or very beautiful. Africa is full of lissom blonde women chasing primates and hyenas for large fees."

"Why do you not apply to the National Geographic?" Hubert asked the two girl botanists graciously.

"Alas," said Maddelena, the plain one, "I cannot interest the Americans in the distribution of heaths in the Coto Doñana."

"And when their grants run out," Patterson raised his voice, "they abandon their proper work and write books."

15

It was unfortunate for me that our mutual dislike was combined with his obsession about books which he considered undeserving money makers. Most evenings he would mention the English-speaking best-seller lists, expressing his disgust at the popularization of ecological themes. He would bore all those who had not heard of the sensational account of pachyderm routine written by the good-looking couple who chose to live among elephants. The scientists around this table were not familiar with the work of the civil servant who had taken the place of Tolkien as a cult figure with his personal interpretation of the behaviour of Berkshire rabbits. They had not heard of the nonagenarian clergyman whose drawings of flowers had earned him a lot of money late in life.

So far I had kept quiet about my own success. But inevitably the time would come when Patterson found out, and now it seemed this had happened.

He had waited for the right conversational opening, "I see," he said to me, "that your own book is still in the lists . . . you can afford to treat yourself to a more appetizing looking dinner."

I had used a *nom-de-plume*, but the television programme prevented anonymity. Also the photographs. "If you have a copy of the book, I'll autograph it," I said, watching him sneer.

"What is this?" asked Lindstrom, blinking behind his thick glasses.

"You did not know," Patterson stated, "that Dr Lacey is the author of a best seller?" Thirteen weeks on the lists, mostly sandwiched between David Niven and a handbook on trees.

"Ah!" said the simple Lindstrom. "That is good, to learn of a scientist of repute earning a lot of money. May I ask what is the subject?"

"It was . . . about swallows . . ."

"But naturally," Luiz Carnera said with Hispanic courtesy, "an authority upon the *Hirundinidae* must write about his speciality . . ."

"*Apodidae*," corrected Patterson. "His field is swifts, not swallows." Carnera was, after all, a hepatologist.

"A study of swallows must be a new departure . . ."

"Cheeky," put in Patterson.

"Please?"

The publishers had insisted on adopting the name Cheeky for

one of the birds that formed the subject of the book. The name they chose for the other was even more dreadful. They claimed they were attracting a reading public with an average mental age of eleven. From them too, had come the title.

I stirred with embarrassment. "It is more or less a photographic record of the difficulties of rearing a late fledging during the winter months."

"Called," persisted the loathsome Patterson, "*A Swallow does not make a Summer*."

There was an uncertain titter round the table. "But this, of course, is not an original experiment?" Lindstrom asked.

"Not at all," I said hastily. "A chance happening combined with a passage from the early autobiography of Colette gave me the idea . . . Surely," I added with a bow to Goncourt, "Colette is one of the most sensitive of writers about natural life." It is as well to keep international relations on a formal level. And I wished to change the subject.

"Colette!" Patterson spoke with great scorn. He may have thought she was a nightclub singer. "I suppose you needed a bit of relaxation after all that fuss about your study of *apodidae*."

"Acclaim more than fuss," protested the good-natured Hubert. "Dr Lacey's admirable observations upon the habits of nestlings of *apus caffer* and *apus unicolor* filled in a gap in ornithological knowledge."

"Hardly enough appeal to the general public to put it in the best-seller lists," Patterson said.

I was not going to explain the series of chances that made me switch from pure to popular science. The sabbatical leave to write up my thesis . . . the Dordogne farmhouse offered rent free by Dorothy's parents . . . the Hassalbad camera . . . Dorothy reading Colette's precise yet fruity prose:

"A whole year of my childhood was devoted to the task of capturing in the kitchen or the cow-house the rare flies of winter for the benefit of two swallows, October nestlings thrown down to us by a gale. Was it not essential to preserve them and to find provender for their insatiable beaks that disdained any but living prey?"

A storm had raged outside the farmhouse as Dorothy read that passage. Next morning, when the wind had lessened, we found a similar situation. The mud nest had blown down on to

17

the Habitat tiles on the converted veranda. The battered fledglings crouched inside, the third brood of the year, pink-fleshed and bare except for the shocking, sparse grey down scattered on their backs and tufted heads. They were reptilian, Jurassic, living lessons in evolution. Their gapes were lemon yellow. Three small Donald Ducks waiting to be fed.

Three was one more than Colette had to deal with, but one died after an exhausting week. Colette did not have a car to help in the task of summoning local school children to catch flies. Small boys were paid to hunt through their father's barns for insects ... live insects.

At five years old Tony could be of little practical help. His task was to be a model. The fledglings photographed well, with Dorothy and Tony, equally photogenic, in attendance. I saw the possibilities at once. A nice easy prose, small endearing creatures in distress. What Colette put into a paragraph I put into fifty thousand words ... the swallows running about under the table like chickens, and later, when they had mastered flight, coming in to land on one's head at a call or a whistle. A charming experience, to be shared by millions ... the book was timed to appear with a brilliantly produced television film. The divorce came afterwards.

"I saw the film," Patterson said. "Lucky that television crew happened to be there at the right time."

He guessed. Some people suspected, and I had a few abusive letters in my fan mail. The idea of a television tie up had been irresistible, and Lansbury was enthusiastic when my agent approached him. He was a film maker with the right quality of ruthlessness.

The second winter in the Dordogne had been an ordeal. We went round the countryside looking for late broods; six or seven nestlings were needed to make sure of continuity. They kept dying, to use an expression, like flies. It proved a bad season for finding the remnants of insect life necessary to keep them alive... and in view of possible adverse publicity we couldn't enlist the help of French schoolboys for a second year.

Dorothy hadn't liked it. I told her that most late nestlings die in any case—they were seldom strong enough to survive the demands of the great migratory journey south. But she thought the whole gruesome episode characteristic of me. She didn't mind

Lansbury posing her against backgrounds carefully matched to my original photographs with small moribund birds clinging to her hair. It was Lansbury who dealt with Tony's temper tantrums, aggravated by the fierce excesses of French primary education, which he had to endure throughout the making of the film. It was a good film, made mostly in wind and hail. Lansbury also found himself a new wife. My agent reckoned that each extra week of our stay in the farmhouse earned me fifteen hundred pounds. The price of my marriage.

Patterson was a canny bastard and nosey as well. I wondered if he had suspicions about other occasions when I had behaved unethically.

The other scientists were also curious. I had been reticent. I have never found it easy to make friends with colleagues, and there was no one here I particularly liked, except perhaps Hubert. And yet most of them respected me because of my work on *apus unicolor*. I had earned myself an international reputation from climbing cliffs on Teneriffe to observe an obscure bird.

"If I may ask," breathed Lindstrom—his curiosity seemed to induce a mist behind his spectacles, "what work are you engaged in here at the present time?"

"Now? Nothing scientific, I'm afraid. Writing for money has begun to fascinate me." I caught Patterson's glowering eye. "I am planning a television programme about the hunter Abel Chapman who stayed in the Coto Doñana during the late nineteenth century."

"Chapman?" asked Patterson. "You mean the heavy that could kill two bustards with a right and left? Four flamingoes with one barrel?"

"Er ... that's right. The programme will coincide with a reissue of his work—and I'm doing an introduction and biographical sketch and so on."

"I wouldn't have thought that in these conservation-minded days a tough like Abel Chapman would make the best-seller lists."

"He wrote travel books that are neglected English classics ... in the spirit of Doughty or Richard Burton." To Patterson, Richard Burton merely meant Elizabeth Taylor's consort.

Old Goncourt surprisingly agreed. "I have perused his *Wild Spain* and *Unexplored Spain* which are here in the library.

Anyone who has the interest of the Coto Doñana at heart must read his work."

I said: "I would like to put Chapman's reputation as a ruthless hunter into perspective. After all, it was accepted custom at the time. Look at Alfonso VII."

Hubert had a memory for figures, useful when counting migratory flocks. "Once his Bourbon majesty shot eighty-three stags, forty-two young bears, fifteen fallow deer and three lynxes all in one day."

"No ecologist," Patterson said. "And Spanish rulers since have kept up the good work. I don't know so much about his grandson, but there was nothing old Franco liked better than killing partridges—for a change."

Dr Horez snapped: "What about the English royal family? They have shot more pheasants than they have shaken hands."

Pablo was raising and lowering a coffee pot and milk jug over my cup like yoyos. Old Goncourt said quickly, "How long are you staying in the place, Dr Lacey?"

Perhaps Patterson's lamented grant would run out by Christmas. No one, not even he, could be continually interested in my movements. "I'll be here till spring," I said.

Lindstrom asked: "And is your project on Abel Chapman all that will occupy you during that time?"

I should have left well alone. "No, I'll be doing some more work on nestlings."

"But surely *apodidae* are only migratory on Doñana?"

"Not *apodidae*," I added hastily—too hastily—"I thought of making some observations on *clamator glandarius*."

"*Clamator glandarius?*" Miguel asked in surprise, and I knew I had made an error. I should have worked out a better cover story. No one in pursuit of original work would touch the great spotted cuckoo. Its dotty habits, contrasting with those of the more familiar *cuculus canorus*, have made it a favourite subject of study. Every amateur old lady bird-watcher knows how it can lay fifteen to sixteen eggs a season and how numbers of eggs can be laid at different intervals in the same nest of its corvid hosts.

"I thought I might try another popular book. Cuckoo fledglings when feathered are appealing. Eric Hosking's famous photograph of a brood of five from a magpie's nest, all of different ages, has a certain aggressive charm. I might photograph a particular nest continually."

Miguel was interested. "You try to catch mother *clamator* at the moment she lays her egg? And baby just as he murders the newborn magpies? The avian equivalent of the infant Hercules strangling the snakes."

"The triumph of the parasite," Patterson said. I wondered at the range of his suspicions. I knew that he had worked as a game warden up in Scotland. Had he also been in wooded country in Breconshire in March, 1972? He added, "Is your photography up to Hosking's?"

"It was adequate for my last book," I said. "With violence and a bit of sex, who knows, I might produce another best seller."

There was a final burst of laughter from the far table as the affluent party got up in a cloud of cigar smoke. Jovial men tottered towards the door, hands clasped around each other's shoulders. Some were absurdly dressed to kill in elegant plus-fours and tailored jackets with leather trimmings.

The naturalists scowled as they went by. "Pollution," muttered Hubert. Only Dr Horez got up and went over to have a deferential word with Don Sanchez. He joined the group as it made its way out towards the drawing room.

"I wouldn't have thought the Maharajah elevated enough for old Horez," Hubert said. "He isn't an aristocrat, is he?" Horez was famous for his snobbery.

"Wealth can elevate your rank, even in Spain," Miguel replied. "Don Sanchez must be one of the richest businessmen in Andalusia."

We lingered sulkily over coffee. When we finally rose and left the dining room we walked along passageways whose walls were cluttered with photographs of ancient hunts. Gentlemen dressed in leather chaps complete with codpieces gazed through binoculars; ladies in dashing sombreros sat knee deep in dead game; sad handsome King Alfonso posed with his vast retinue.

In the drawing room Don Sanchez's guests were assembled under a dark portrait of Philip IV, occasionally giving out bursts of loud laughter while Dr Horez directed Pablo to bring balloon glasses of brandy. For centuries courtiers had listened to the conversation of kings in this very spot. The rest of us settled down glumly in antlered chairs playing chess or reading the available literature that included Abel Chapman's works or rarities like an old Journal of the Bombay Historical Society. Alternatively there were a couple of *Playboys* which Patterson had smuggled into Spain.

One of the kerosene lamps blinked, and behind the bars of the window a ghostly wind shook the leaves of the eucalyptus groves, making them rattle like knife blades. Then we could hear rain drumming on the parched ground.

The rest of the night was chaotic. Doors and windows banged; some of us rushed about in the rain, shouting and waking up the palace servants. Don Sanchez's guests wanted their cars brought round before the storm got worse, while the naturalists demanded lights and torches. A stork broke its wing and had to be rescued from a windswept tree; Hubert handled it with a fine gentleness as he took it in from the storm. Patterson had been whiling away moments of idleness during the drought by taming a half-grown buzzard; this was now swept away in a tangle of leather and feathers. It vanished over the marshes, never to return, all its new tameness blown out of it by the wind. The bonds knotted round its talons ensured a quick death.

Next morning the barns and outhouses behind the palace had become refuges for thousands of late migrating birds. Here was an opportunity for Horez to direct a day's entertainment and take over the job of the resident ringers. Under his orders the staff, including the girls from the kitchen, chased the unfortunate victims of the storm into nets. Shrieking with laughter, they went around jabbing under the eaves, armed with poles and flashlights. As the bewildered swallows, who had already been mobbed by the resident starlings, were dislodged and netted, one could not help being aware of their obvious terror. I speculated if it increased when they were transferred to Horez's control. He stood waiting for them with a large cloth bag, and it was difficult to tell from the door poacher's expression on his face whether he was about to wring their necks or ring their feet.

Chapter two

I T WAS A physical pleasure to see rain spilling down unrelentingly on the dusty surfaces of Doñana. Over the hard powdery crust of the dried-up marshland pools began to form and spread. Little by little they blended into a great translucent lake of tawny-coloured water. Life returned. The geese had been harbingers of the autumn migration. Now clouds of water-birds began to come in—teal, pintail, shoveler, widgeon, mallard in huge numbers, scoter and garganey. They were winter visitors who would not be breeding here. I would have to wait until January before any birds began to think of nesting. Perhaps when I thought out this expedition I had been too cautious in establishing myself here at the beginning of autumn. But for a rich and homeless ornithologist without a proper scientific programme to occupy him, the *Estación* was a pleasant enough place to pass the winter. Besides, there was Abel Chapman, the nineteenth-century hunter; I had a contract to write about him.

I could not work at Chapman as intently as I would have liked; the subject was sometimes depressing. A man whose clear powers of observation and vivid style of writing led merely to counting corpses inevitably became tedious. The weight of dead flesh he accumulated was oppressive; you could not help feeling the waste in the recorded slaughter. After reading a nauseating passage describing the shooting of scores of different species of birds during a morning's exercise, one could only abandon his powerful narrative for the day.

I found myself entering casually into the routine of the resident naturalists. Observing my colleagues I could abandon Chapman from time to time and write the odd article about ornithology for the popular press. I began to take my turn of going down to the nets and examining the night's catches. Nothing much during the winter months—a couple of chiff chaffs, a stonechat or two. I'd put these into pouches and bring them to the ringing room where details were recorded about length of wing, weight and age, determined, if the bird was a male, by the length of its penis. Then the slender rings had to be fitted gently around its foot, after which it was released through the barred window. December and January were dull times for this sort of work. In spring and summer, when scores of different species arrived each day, the ringers really got down to business; the nets had to be examined every hour or so and the recording of names and numbers took a lot of time. On Doñana they tab something like fourteen thousand birds a year. My contribution was small, but I enjoyed those early-morning hours wandering round the palace. When you were near to it, the proportions loomed, but it gave no impression of oppressive grandeur. The sun dappled four neatly arranged palm trees in the small courtyard. Glistening white walls and bougainvillaea suggested tourists' Spain. The chapel was modest, and so, too, was the miniature bull ring where members of the Medina Sidonia family had enjoyed their private sports. When Philip IV visited them in 1624, he stood on the balcony of the Casa de Bosque and shot three running bulls with his harquebus. The palace was made for blood and games, where men could kill without recourse to war. Abel Chapman was only one of a long tradition.

I did a number of tours, mainly by myself, sometimes with Hubert or Miguel, ambling about, learning the geography of the Coto, experiencing the pleasure that the place must give anyone who loves birds. Hubert's job was making up statistics—basically counting. As spring approached, the more exotic species began to arrive—spoonbill, feathery little crab herons, rarities like ferruginous and white-headed duck.

Patterson had also stayed on for the winter. Like myself he had to wait for the right season. His speciality was courtship—how he persuaded his university or whoever was paying for him to let him come to Doñana in the early autumn was his own affair. It was January before he could indulge in his particular form of voyeurism—watching randy ducks. His other pastime was needling me. When we met socially—which was every evening—he kept up the inquisitive banter that first made us enemies. I tried to preserve a frozen politeness. The others ignored the tenseness between us, which only once broke into a quarrel when I discovered that he was questioning Hubert about my daily routine.

By January there were quite a lot of new people to observe

our bickering. Many of the old ones had left. Goncourt had found his pondweed and taken it to Paris. Lindstrom, Heller, the two girl botanists and the scruffy Smith had gone. Espinar left in the New Year. Other specialists took their places. This change was inevitable; like so many of the birds in the wilderness, the scientists in the palace were by definition migrants. Of those left from October there were Dr Horez—more or less resident—Hubert, Miguel, the ringers, myself, and to my infinite regret, Patterson.

The palace welcomed other creatures of passage. Huntsmen came down, mostly from Madrid and Seville. Of course they were not allowed to shoot on *Estación* land, but there was plenty of space outside it; meanwhile the palace made a pleasant, if expensive, place where they could find entertainment. Frequently their host was Don Sanchez. His particular guests, inevitably nicknamed The Children of Sanchez, somehow seemed larger, richer, noisier than the others, the ones with the most expensive guns and the largest amount of dead deer. Once they dined on a boar's head which one of them had shot—it was served with patterns of parsley, lemon and mayonnaise tattooing its features and a Golden Delicious apple in its mouth. Hubert, who hated Sanchez to the point of mania, emphasized the refinement of his vulgarity.

"It isn't as if he didn't have his own hunting lodge every bit as elaborate as this place. There are only three in the whole area —*Las Marismillas* belonging to the Dukes of Tarifa, this palace, and his own—*Las Marismas Negras*. Why doesn't he entertain there?"

"Perhaps we've got a better cook in Maria. Perhaps he wants to show his friends off to us and to Horez."

"I don't see why Horez finds him such entertainment. It can't be merely an exercise in snobbery. That useful prefix Don ..."

"Gentleman, esquire, chevalier ... why not? You're a snob yourself."

"Sanchez is self-made. Started by owning a small bar in Seville ..."

"I know ..." We'd listened to local gossip ... how he had clawed his way to success with the aid of astute connections—business and Falangist ... Sometimes on winter evenings it had been pleasant to talk about a subject totally unconnected with ornithology. "And now he has rice plantations, resort hotels, Seville apartment houses, a ranch or two of fighting bulls . . ."

"The most popular recreation of the wealthy in Andalusia," Hubert said, "is arranging the ritual slaughter of bulls. Not a direct exercise in violence—that is the province of the matador. But the rich will indulge in the dangerous killing of deer . . ."

"You really do loathe him."

"I hate anyone who shoots for sport."

"It seems ironic that you of all people should be named after the patron saint of huntsmen."

"So my family repeatedly points out. I asked Horez about Sanchez, and he said that he was forming a consortium. Ignorant fools like Horez, whenever they encounter a group of rich men, always start talking about consortiums . . ."

That last morning had promised well, a golden day in spring. Winter had departed and the breeding season was well established.

Breakfast had been the usual casual affair in the kitchen. Pablo and one of the girls grilled the *tostado* which was covered with a jam and served up with Nescafé. There were a few variations to the menu. Patterson's five hundred tea bags were still holding out, while Martín, an eccentric Castilian entymologist, insisted on ritually pouring hot water over a disgusting white powder from a packet called *Suenos de oro*, maintaining that the hot lemonade kept him awake and active.

On this last field trip with Hubert I packed with more than usual care the little khaki bag that had once belonged to my father and once contained a gas mask. After some hesitation I wrapped a pair of climbing irons in newspaper and put them in first. Then a small polystyrene box. I added a field guide to European birds—the ornithologist's ready reckoner—a graphed notebook, several sharpened pencils, a sharpener, an unopened packet of Rothmans and a book of matches. Pablo provided me with some of my own salami, a roll of bread and two oranges. I zipped a roll of money into the pouch of my anorak and hung round my neck the new toy which had given me pleasure all winter—the Zeiss binoculars which were one of the few luxuries I acquired when the royalties from my book first came in . . . 10 × 40 Dailyt central focusing, their twilight performance excellent, the precision of their daylight powers about the best money could buy. A firm in Essex had charged me a hundred and thirty pounds for them.

Hubert waited for me outside the arched entrance of the palace. There was the usual morning stir. Three guides waited on horseback, prepared to lead newcomers to Doñana on a tour. That meant that no one this morning had felt opulent enough to hire the Land Rover to go cross country. Romero and Jaime looked pleased about this, since the Land Rover deprived them of work and tips; the third rider, Antonio, seemed to be sulking, probably because he was usually assigned as driver for the motorized trips.

Juan, one of the ringers, was attending to the wants of the small menagerie kept in wire cages under the eucalyptus grove. A wolf, the mongoose Josefina, and two wild dogs were being fed to the jeers of the resident raven, a noted stealer of jewellery from women scientists. After hopping around the ground with its characteristic jerky movements seeking discarded morsels, it flew off to the kitchen in search of something more sustaining.

Immediately around the palace a light wind shook the beautiful specimen trees that had been brought over from South America more than a century ago. They were well named *bella sombre*. Their great feathery branches, which provided nesting sites for anything from golden orioles to kites, nodded over the white building and surrounding flat land. Along the edge of the *marismas* a herd of red deer stood reflected in pools of water beneath a mass of rose-coloured clouds. Red sky at morning *vaquero*'s warning? Romero, Jaime and Antonio evidently thought so; their grey sombreros were fitted with waterproof covers, and black capes were tied in neat bundles across the pommels of their saddles.

Hubert and I took the Martinazo trail along the edge of the *marismas*. They stretched to the far horizon, blending to form a vast shallow lake flecked with cattle egrets. Here and there in the water the green tips of reeds or patches of sedge showed through, meagre grazing for cattle and wild horses. The path, which followed a line of cork trees, was made up of thick sand. Whenever one travels in Doñana one is reminded of its recent maritime origins. We saw pieces of broken shell, and the sand, which supported coarse grass and aromatic bushes, seemed to be of the finest golden seaside variety. The air resounded to the singing, whistling and hoarse cries of birds who were nest building. They stirred perpetually as we moved. Hubert walked ahead of me with the slow unhurried pace of the experienced bird-watcher. Occasionally he stopped to raise his binoculars, and I would follow suit in a manoeuvre that was almost military. We saw nothing out of the ordinary—the occasional yellow flash of an oriole, some magpies and a lot of warblers—there are twenty-two different species to be found in the area. Larks were also abundant, woodlarks mostly, although I once spotted something a little different, and we both stopped to follow the flight of a grey bird with a brown streaked breast.

"*Galerida cristata* or *galerida thecklae*?" murmured Hubert. I had no idea whether it was a crested lark or Theckla's. Hubert was sure it was a crested, and we argued a bit about whether it was at all possible to tell the two species apart just by a sighting. Latin has to survive as a *lingua franca* among scientists; otherwise any international conversation about—say—a lesser short-toed lark—would prove a struggle. The Spanish have several different names for larks—*calendria, terrera, cogujada* and so forth, and no name at all for a bird like *calandrella raytal*, a vagrant which they have never even noticed.

Once Hubert raised his glasses higher into the sky; he had spotted a change from the usual circling kite.

"*Gyps fulvus. Magnifique!*"

The griffon vulture sailed on its ragged wings, its long bare neck, white ruffle and curved beak clearly visible through binoculars. See one vulture at work and you've seen them all, though of course they vary in numbers and style. Not a pretty sight—a hissing mob, all blood, feathers and rubbery necks specially developed by evolution for digging deep into stomach walls.

Hubert asked: "Did you read that report about Indian vultures growing more fastidious? About householders in high-rise flats overlooking the Farsi towers of silence on the outskirts of Bombay? There have been complaints that vultures can no longer be relied on to dispose of corpses."

"Obviously they consider Bombay garbage more succulent."

"A change in behaviour pattern comparable to that of seagulls leaving the sea for refuse dumps."

"I would have thought that the towers of silence would provide a more restricted diet than the sea."

"But readily available."

28

"One would have to investigate the death rate among Farsis."

It took about an hour's walk to reach the Hafner Hide. Many parts of the palace or the estate had been named after distinguished huntsmen—the King's suite, the Duke's Fountain, the room of El Conde del Merito. The new occupiers had adapted this pleasant custom in a different form, and the wooden hut we were approaching bore the name of an ornithologist named Henri Hafner.

Any birds in the marsh scattered while we entered and settled ourselves. After a little time things got back to normal, and through the narrow slits in the hide we watched some moorhens. In the distance a large red kite soared above the tree where it was building its nest.

"You know how *milvus* often has a piece of old cloth in its nest?" Hubert said.

"Shakespeare's Autolycus mentions it in *The Winter's Tale*. "My traffic is sheets; when the kite builds, look to lesser linen . . ."

"Of course kites were common over European cities in his day. Do you still have them in England?"

"A small colony of *milvus milvus* is confined to Wales. I have observed it there." I grinned.

"Something amuses you?"

I thought there would be no harm in telling Hubert. "A couple of years ago I climbed up to . . . er . . . examine an old nest—and do you know what I discovered? The remains of an old T-shirt with a picture on it of the Bay City Rollers."

"Who are the Bay City Rollers?"

By the time I had explained Hubert was concentrating his attention on a pair of red shanks. Sitting in the stuffy little cupboard was uncomfortable, but better than wading in marsh and hiding behind bulrushes. A hoopoe fluttered over to our left, then some cattle egrets moved among the marshes. Our range of vision included water and land. Hubert recorded the sighting of a Sardinian warbler—the first of the year. Later he nabbed a singing blackbird for his book, a great tit, and wrote again as he noticed a bright-coloured bee eater fresh from Ethiopia. ("You have none in England?" "I believe a pair bred in Sussex about twenty years ago.") Then he heard a great spotted cuckoo. That was the moment that Patterson entered the hide. The place seemed very crowded and stuffy and I suggested lunch.

29

"Outside?"

The swamp mud on Patterson's clothes was unpleasant. Hubert said: "Very well." We moved some distance from the hide and sat lounging beside the water gazing at the double images of reflected egrets.

"*Clamator glandarius*, eh?" Patterson was going through Hubert's notes. "I thought that was going to be your new life work, Lacey?"

"Oh, I don't seem to have the time to get away from Abel Chapman. Later if I can find some nests they've taken over I might try and get photographs."

"You might miss a few photographic opportunities today, being without your camera," Hubert said.

"No hurry," I said. "Magpies' nests are common enough."

"The dedicated ornithologist," Patterson said.

"Today I'm relaxing. Wasting time like you." Our emergence from the hide had put an end to serious watching for the moment.

"Does *clamator glandarius* parasitize any other species in Doñana besides magpies?" asked Hubert.

"Apparently not. In Africa it likes to use the nests of *corvus corone*." I was tired of this conversation; in fact I knew very little about these blasted cuckoos. "What can you see?" I asked Patterson, who was lying on his back looking upwards through his binoculars. Suddenly he sat up and snatched at my bag, taking out the field guide.

"Do you mind? I want to check if those are Egyptian vultures."

"Help yourself." I wondered if he saw the climbing irons.

Hubert also turned his lenses towards the black dots in the sky. "*Neophron Percnopterus*? Certainly that is what they are, though they are flying too high to see their yellow faces." Vultures can soar fifteen thousand feet up and more. He reached for his notebook.

"Haven't you got your own guide?" I asked Patterson.

"Don't really need it at present. I'm concentrating on white storks."

"At the Algaida? I'm going along there now." I had planned it earlier with Hubert. You don't need two watchers in the same place. The Algaida was a heronry established in the region known as the Belotta Gorda; at this time of year the sky above the ancient cork oaks where the birds nested resembled a raging snowstorm. Besides little egrets and cattle egrets, the numerous species of heron made up the largest breeding colony in Europe.

"Don't mess up my birds," Patterson said. He behaved as if he owned white storks. He resented anyone else watching their courtship display and noting how they would stand and face each other, bowing like dancers doing a gavotte. They would clapper their bills and inflate their small crimson throat pouches as they swayed gracefully from side to side. I hoped very much that if he had just been to the Algaida, he'd hardly want to go back again.

He had indeed. "I was there at dawn. It's really the only time to get proper viewings."

"One or two dancing storks will be quite enough for me," I said, getting up.

Hubert said, "Wait. I need a diversion when I go back into the hide." Birds are not good at counting; if two people entered the hide and one left noisily, most of them would assume that it had become empty.

Patterson hesitated. If he had made some good sightings that morning at the heronry, he would want to get back to write them up. Several times during the past week he had had to make a choice—whether to get on with his own work, or to keep in touch with my activities. He did not quite have the neck to voice his suspicions without some sort of proof.

"I'll do the diversion if Lacey wants to get along."

I left them and walked through a still landscape of ancient cork oaks dotted around the edge of the marsh water which was glassy under the perpetual reflected sky. I went nowhere near the Algaida. Instead I turned off before reaching the Guard's House to make my way through a patch of scrub beside the *marismas*. Over the water in the distance the cluster of trees surrounding the palace showed clearly—a landmark for miles around.

The cork tree I was aiming for stood isolated from the others. It was conspicuous enough with its three huge branches and canopy of silver green leaves. But the huge raft of sticks supported on top which had accumulated over the past weeks made it stand out even more.

I had carefully checked the schedule of scientists and tourists staying at the palace, and the jobs that the guards and staff were supposed to be doing. I had followed the plans of other ornithologists for the day. Of course they were changeable. An hour would be enough to complete the job; after that I would be able to drift to the heronry as I said I would. The real trouble was Patterson. I looked back over a couple of miles of scrubland and searched with my binoculars. No sign of movement that I could see.

Was it worth taking the risk? Why not come back another time? But tomorrow they were going to start building the hide beside the cork oak, step by step in easy stages. It would be completed in time for the hatching of fledglings. Some Danes were due to arrive next week and film for television, and they wanted their nice comfortable hide ready for them. Today was one of the few chances that I would have. I could have risked it a few days earlier, but from the observation I had made, I knew it would be profitless to try too soon.

The distance from the ground to the nest looked about sixty feet, a perpendicular ascent. With the climbing irons I thought that it would take me about ten minutes to get to the underside of the nest. Then there would be some problems. From the patch of juniper where I studied my objective carefully, I could see the head of the female and her curved bill, the colour of smoked glass, strong enough to carry a full-grown rabbit. The sandy black sheen of her crown set off her mad golden eye. Far above her I could see her mate—a grown adult bird, perhaps two or three years old, with distinctive white markings and chocolate plumage quartering the sky. Wings extended, gliding, effortlessly moving in great circles. And then I heard its hoarse bark, a resonant "Owk owk" as it made signals of approaching danger.

Unlike most other predators the Spanish imperial eagle disdains to nest in remote mountain eyries, and is fool enough to live openly on the plains. Its monster nest, which it painstakingly resites and rebuilds every year, can be seen for miles around. *Aquila heliaca adalberti*, one of the most handsome of European eagles, coloured like a chocolate cake with white icing, is a subspecies of the imperial eagle, and one of the rarest birds in Europe. Out of a total of perhaps fifty birds in all Spain about eight or ten nest on Doñana. It is a bird that is inevitably doomed to extinction.

I would only take one egg from the clutch.

There would be two or perhaps three—short elliptical to short subelliptical. They would be white to pale buff, newspaper-coloured, with sparse markings of brown, grey or purple. No gloss on their surface. Their size about that of a large hen's egg.

Of the fledglings that hatched, in all probability only one would survive to get the undivided attention of its parents. I would be saving a fair amount of misery.

But Hubert's simple dictum during that dinner table discussion a few months ago would always hold. "They are scum." I was lower than scum. I knew my position. The ultimate betrayal is that of the ornithologist who collects black eggs. I publicly proclaimed my belief in conservation. I didn't even have a scientific excuse, like the oologist in America who was a receiver of stolen raptor's eggs because he wanted to study the protein content of their albumen. I was merely drugged like an anaesthetist who becomes addicted to the narcotic he deals with.

Outside England eggs are mostly stolen to be eaten. To obtain them for, let us say, aesthetic purposes, is considered a peculiarly English pastime like sodomy used to be. Of course nowadays it is regarded as a far worse crime. The Royal Society for the Protection of Birds reckons that there are about two hundred active collectors in Great Britain. When they are caught magistrates fine them the maximum. A man from Coventry was recently fined a hundred and fifty-five pounds plus a hundred pounds costs for stealing from a peregrine's nest; another from Hereford seventy-five pounds, plus a hundred and fifty pounds costs, for taking kites' eggs. I have a good clutch of kites' eggs myself.

People think of egg thieves as retired Colonel Blimps who got their values all wrong during their childhood by reading the *Boy's Own Paper* and mixing up the Boy Scout oath. A few of these are left, but they are a dying breed; the dawn chorus on the south coast sounds louder and clearer after the obituary columns of the *Brighton Herald* and the *Sussex Gazette* have gone to press. Those that survive are active old gentlemen, perfectly capable of organizing a commando raid up a Scottish crag or a Welsh pine, and not, as they are sometimes pictured, too doddery to leave their firesides and receiving their loot from feeble-minded gamekeepers and sub-human poachers. There are other egg stealers, a younger crowd altogether. Not that I know

33

any. It's a solitary obsession; we do not have reunions to compare trophies. We are outcasts. When Abel Chapman aimed his rifle at booted eagles and imperial eagles, he could shoot them with a light heart and a clean conscience, because he regarded them as vermin. Today in a ravished world birds are a diminishing asset. There are fewer than there used to be.

One man the RSPB prosecuted had twenty-six thousand eggs in his possession. This seems greedy. When there is no avian life left in this world, apart from pigeons and seagulls and the quelea, the weaver bird whose nesting colonies have taken over large parts of Africa, my own collection will be something like three thousand eggs. They are all special. A short spring holiday most years has brought me opportunities to break the law relating to "wilful disturbance" of rare birds' nests. Buff subelliptical booty from a colony of avocets. A smooth white biconical clutch lifted from the rotting vegetation that makes up the nest of the Slavonian grebe. Brown short subelliptical non-glossy nestling holders from a merlin's moorland nursery. Olive and blotched markings from the shallow shingle bed of little tern. More recently I have stolen abroad. Madeira and the Dordogne did not produce very much, but I managed a June trip to Iceland, and not so long ago a quick profitable holiday on the Danube delta. And now a leisurely season on Doñana.

The colours of birds' eggs are probably derived from waste products in the blood stream passing into the oviduct. They usually have an evolutionary explanation. Camouflage is one; for instance the speckled markings on the creamy and buff backgrounds of terns' eggs make them inconspicuous in the stony places where they are laid. The freshly laid blue-white eggs of grebes and dab chicks gradually become less noticeable as the parent covers them with rotten weed that stains them a yellowish colour every time it leaves its nest. Other birds like something more visible; hole nesters generally have white eggs they can see in the dark. Crows' eggs, laid in the open, are blotched, while jackdaws, who are beginning to lay in concealed places, are tending to produce whiter eggs. Cuckoos make an evolutionary choice of hosts, and their eggs vary. Some end up in a wrong-coloured nest because of overcrowding; and it can happen that a meadow pipit type of cuckoo egg has to go into a garden warbler's home.

Guillemots have an incredible range of colour in their eggs. Guillemots nest in colonies, so that it is important for an individual to recognize what she has laid and not get muddled. Her egg will not only be different in colour from that of her neighbours; it will be pyroform to prevent it from falling off cliffs, an essential modification of ledge-nesting colonies.

Why do gannets and flamingoes have soft chalky stained eggs? Round, oval, elliptical, pyroform, white, buff pastel, stained, speckled, blotched, glossy. The range of colouring is subtle, like William Blake's palette. The eggs of some waders resemble photographs of the earth taken by astronauts. The scrawled eggs of Cretzschmar's Bunting could have been marked by Jackson Pollock.

Eggs last. They may lose some of their pristine gloss, but they will always retain their essential beauty. At Tring, the British Museum's Natural History headquarters, they have an egg of a glaucous gull collected in 1817 ... still smooth with a slightly granular surface, buff with spotted markings.

Dorothy found out that I stole birds' eggs and from then on behaved as if I habitually dressed up in her clothes.

Patterson suspected. Many hysterical RSPB types can spot egg collectors more easily than rare avian species.

I swept my binoculars round the pale flat landscape to check that I was alone. The tree had a welcome pool of shade spreading under its branches—didn't Cervantes eulogize a cork tree for just this reason? I was an experienced climber, not only as a result of robbing remotely positioned nests. My legitimate scientific activities had entailed several years of cliff and mountain climbing. Swift colonies in Teneriffe are in inaccessible places, which is why their nursery habits remained a mystery for so long.

This tree presented some variable hazards. For the first twenty feet the bark had been stripped off to make corks for sherry bottles, which meant that the surface, instead of being rough and corrugated, was smooth and slippery as if it had been greased. Then there was another thirty feet of bark before the branches shot out, brazier-like, to hold the nest. With other birds it is usually an easy enough matter, once the nest is reached, to slip your hand inside and take the eggs. But predators present unusual problems, the most immediate being the overhang of the nest; it is like climbing round the underside of a toadstool, on top of which is a very angry gnome. At least there were no electronic listening devices like those surrounding the osprey's nest at Loch Garten.

The climbing irons were lightweight aluminium, much the same design as those used by post office workers. Even with their help it was difficult to get a grip on the smooth hard inner skin of the cork tree. Progress was slow, and I spent a slippery six or seven minutes before reaching the rough bark and getting a good firm grip. This was time enough for the female eagle to become really agitated, and although I could not see her when I gazed up at the mass of twigs that made up the bottom of the nest, I could hear her frenzied warning signal—a sharp "Owk owk" that sounded like the firing of shot. In due course I would have to face both enraged birds, when a thrust of a powerful wing might conceivably dislodge me and send me toppling sixty feet to the ground. But my immediate worry was that these loud cries could be heard over a considerable distance. Any wandering guard could recognize them as cries of distress, and ornithologists would come running.

I hurried to accomplish the manoeuvre which Abel Chapman once compared to "scaling the futtock shroud of an old line of battleship". (Chapman thought nothing of trampling over nests and destroying fledglings.) The eagle's behaviour was the equivalent of a storm at sea. She was hissing now, as well as screaming and jumping up and down as I twisted my legs round one of the protruding branches, leaned out, grabbed the edge of the platform and looked over the top. Pieces of litter and twigs rained down on my head. Now I could see across the raft of branches and pinecones, some of which were still green, because the nest had only been completed a few days before. It was already mucky, covered with droppings and bones. Among them stood the eagle, handsome in her sable plumage, set off by white epaulettes on each wing. Above her head whirled her husband shrieking abuse. She hopped towards me, bouncing heavily on the nest's surface, so that I thought the whole thick contraption might give way and I would fall with it. But it held; it was firm enough for her to make stabbing darts at me with her beak and talons, her head moving from side to side so that each golden eye in turn gave me a contemptuous stare.

I avoided the beak, but a talon rippled my left arm. Blood

36

flowed out easily. I hauled myself on to the platform and she retreated, hissing and screaming. I pelted her with sticks. For the first time in my egg-stealing career I wished I had not scorned the common naturalist's technique of quieting a ferocious bird—throwing a cloth over it as if it were a budgie cheeping too loud. I had considered such action unsporting. Now the male looked as if he was closing in.

If there had been a fledgling they would have put up more of a fight. But eggs were inanimate treasure. I heard a great whoosh of wings as the female toppled off the nest in a shallow dive and then rose to join her mate angrily zig-zagging a couple of hundred feet above me.

Chapter three

I LOOKED INTO the faint depression lined with fine twigs, dried grass and leaves. Both eagles had spent months constructing their smelly nursery with an air of weary concentration. I had watched them on numerous occasions before completing my plans. There were two eggs. I wanted both of them. The sparse brown markings on one varied with the other which had a good deal of freckling—unusual on eggs of the imperial eagle, although I knew that it had been noted a number of times among golden eagles. I stared at them for nearly half a minute, while cries sounded above my head and blood from my hand flowed on to the chewed remains of a rabbit. I sweated, for it was very hot up here on the open platform exposed to the sun. There seemed to be enough heat for incubation to take place without the parent sitting at all. A fledgling, wrapped in his down, would need the temperament of a salamander to endure the fiercer suns of April and May.

Reminding myself yet again that there were less than a hundred Spanish imperial eagles in existence, I stretched out my uninjured hand over bits of feather, old bones and regurgitated pellets of food, and gently pilfered the freckled egg. A Rembrandt among birds' eggs.

It fitted snugly into the reinforced polystyrene box I had prepared. This went into the pouch of my anorak. I slipped over the side of the great raft and perched on one of the curved supporting branches underneath. Here I was relatively safe from the hovering furious eagles. It was unlikely that they would swoop in to attack me now. Probably, if she followed the patterns of raptor psychology that I had observed, the female would get over her agitation in due course. She would resume sitting on the surviving egg. When I robbed the Speyside osprey's nest, I substituted a large hen's egg taken from a Sainsbury pack. It deceived the osprey for weeks; she brooded until those who were guarding her grew impatient and came to take a look. These eagles' eggs were bigger than hens' and I had not contemplated a similar deception. But since a bird's counting faculties are so limited, with a bit of luck the female *aquila heliaca* would not miss the absence of one. She would swear at me a few more times and then return. Of course the hide that was due to be built might further disturb her. It would have been kinder of me to select another nest—but I had been unable to locate another which did not present every kind of inconvenience.

I lingered on the branch some time before attempting the descent. The eagles cries continued to be shrill, emphasizing my socially vulnerable position. It had been difficult to select the best time for my enterprise. In the British Isles daybreak on a chilly March morning is usually a moment when you can expect to find yourself alone. But in Spain the peasant or labourer is on his way to work at that time, which was why the lethargy of siesta had seemed safer, and I had planned my raid during the great afternoon pause.

One has to take some risks, but the thought of Patterson nagged me. I had brought my binoculars up the tree with me, not as a conscious decision, but because it had not occurred to me to make the physical action of lifting them off my neck. Binoculars are as important to an ornithologist as a gun is to a Los Angeles cop. He carries them all the time he is outdoors. There is a permanent groove on the back of the neck, worn by the strap.

My hand was still bleeding, the drops falling down sixty feet to the sand. I put the binoculars to my eyes, making the minute ocular adjustments automatically, and began a quick periscope sweep around me.

Half the world was water. The reflection from the still marshes helped the dazzling effects of light and shade varying across the surface of the golden plain. The clear light and faintly grotesque trees gave the wild landscape an artificial look. There was an odd air of cultivation about the naked cork trees, stripped to their shoulders, and the flat stone pines that floated above the marshes looking like the solid clouds in Persian miniatures. Even from up here you noticed the birds—egrets, a heron slipping over the water, flapping its wings with a deceptively lazy beat, a couple of swooping magpies, and some distance away, a little movement that looked like grains of sand being thrown up in the air that must have been a flock of partridge.

What had disturbed them? There was a man there, moving with big strides through some undergrowth towards the edge of the water. I could only see bits of him as the heath and scrub protected him from full view. Could he be Patterson? Damn him, why couldn't he mind his own business? But what was he doing coming from over there The last time I had seen him was way over to my left to the east. Even if he had sprinted after me with the speed of an Olympic runner, he could scarcely have got around to the spot where I was viewing him. I could only see him patchily behind the great bushes of thorn and heath. Of course he wasn't Patterson—I was obsessed by him. This was a black-haired man, a Mediterranean type as opposed to Patterson's sandy Celtic colouring.

A stranger was just as unwelcome. The people who lived here were used to eccentricities on the part of bird-watchers, but someone who was up a cork tree crouching under an eagle's nest would arouse comment. Naturally I was wearing inconspicuous clothes—a dirty green anorak and khaki trousers. But the screaming eagles were above me. He paid no attention to them. Undoubtedly he was within earshot; they could be heard for miles, probably as far away as the Hafner Hide. But he continued to stroll towards the water. He was preoccupied. I shifted the Zeiss over to the right a couple of inches.

The group at the edge of the *marismas* had a very stagey appearance, partly because the windless clarity of the swamp water behind them seemed like a painted backcloth. Partly also, that for the first couple of seconds after I picked out the three men and the four horses there was no movement from any of them. Then one of the horses began nodding its head up and down.

They were not really immobile. It was just that one man was concentrating on tying a stone to the feet of a second who was lying prone. The third watched. Both the upright men were young; the one who was fiddling with the rope was scarcely more than a boy. His Moorish features put me in mind of an American juvenile delinquent. Black curly hair protruded from a scarf wrapped round his head and tied tightly beneath his chin so that it looked like a balaclava. On top of the scarf was an old half sombrero. His brown coat was slightly ragged with bulging mis-shapen pockets. He wore gumboots.

His companion had gumboots too. The rest of him had much more of a grey grubby look so that it was difficult to tell the real colour of his clothes. He seemed to have some dirty occupation, a sweep or a coal miner. He might have been a charcoal burner. His prominent Roman nose and thin mouth, contrasting with the full lips of his companion, gave him a purposeful expression that put me in mind of a gannet. The Zeiss could pick out stubble on his cheek. A Saturday night shave had probably been his last. The Moor, too, was unshaven.

The man who lay on the ground was older. I grasped this fact before it occurred to me that he was dead. The deduction that he was dead came last of all, because meanwhile I recognized him. The baggy corduroy trousers, black leather riding jacket and slouched hat belonged to the uniform of the *guardias* who paced Doñana on horseback. I recognized Jaime, whom I had seen a few hours before, early in the morning as I set out for the Hafner with Hubert. His hat still had its waterproof covering. Jaime was the oldest of the palace guards, the stodgy one who was considered the most reliable because of his experience. When celebrities or important visitors came to the palace his suggestions for expeditions were taken seriously. Younger naturalists liked him less than the gay feckless Romero or Antonio with his wisecracks. But they wouldn't have wished to see him now.

The fourth man joined the group. He was shaking his head, a counterpoint in movement to the horse. Perhaps he had been looking for another stone? Or another place to bury Jaime? But what would be better than the *cano* in front of them?

Recognition is a strange thing. I had known Jaime instantly, but it was not until I saw this stranger's jodhpurs that I identified him. He was Don Sanchez—the Maharajah, entertainer, hunter and Hubert's *bête-noire*. He was making imperious gestures, telling them to get on with it. A Spaniard's gestures are used sparingly, unlike an Italian's, and even in the frenzy of hurry there was something stately about this fat man's movements. The others moved quickly. The *cano* must have been some yards away from the edge of the quiet water. *Canos* are deep holes that occur here and there beneath the surface of the *marismas*.

They can be death traps if you are on horseback, wading knee deep, although a good horse will sense one if you let him have his head. Some of the most obvious and notorious are marked by keep away notices ornamented with skulls and crossbones.

The horse they chose for the task must have been an experienced *marismas* horse in spite of his nondescript appearance. A skinny, sleepy chestnut, I thought that it was Jaime's. I seemed to remember the blue check saddlebag resting on its withers upon a piece of white plastic behind the high curved saddle which was virtually a howdah. The crupper that held this seat in place looked like a pair of braces.

The charcoal burner, assisted by the Moor, heaved Jaime up in front of the beaked pommel. Because of the weight of the stones tied to his feet, most of him hung down the horse's left side, his hands swinging well below the heavy Spanish stirrup, which was solid metal, shaped like a paper boat. It swung as the horse moved, giving Jaime a blow on the cheek. I could see his grave face upside down. There was a white weal across his forehead from the shadow of his hat, worn at the same rakish angle for several decades. It still stayed on, held in place by its leather strap. Above I could see a tear in his jacket. A bullet hole? A stab wound?

The charcoal burner got up behind him. He sat awkwardly because of the peculiar weight distribution, but from the way that he urged the horse into the water it was plain that he was a good rider. The water came up to the horse's knees; the stirrups dipped and rippled on the surface. Jaime's head, arms and shoulders became completely submerged; for a few instants the wash they created had a slightly different tinge, a gravy colour. Blood. Twice the horse stopped and hesitated; then the arch of Jaime's headless body would be reflected, making a double curve like a cupid's bow.

There was no sign when they reached the edge of the *cano* except that the animal's increasing hesitation became a stubborn stop, and, but for the weight it was carrying, it would have started to rear and plunge. The charcoal burner somehow coaxed it to turn round forty-five degrees so that Jaime's feet came into view round the other side. As an exhibition of dressage the manoeuvre would not have disgraced that white-horsed tourist place in Vienna. Then he took out a knife from his belt, flicked it open and began to saw through the rope that bound Jaime to the saddle. The horse stood rigid, its legs at all angles, like a rocking horse. The ropes were cut, and, as the weight of the stones took him away, Jaime's head emerged from the water briefly for the last time. His hat was still on. His arms came up next with a wave, as they disappeared over the saddle pommel. I couldn't see him go underwater into the *cano* because the horse was in the way.

I had been watching for about five minutes, and had taken in all that detail with the concentration of a man who sets out to memorize a trayful of objects. Viewing through the Zeiss gave me a feeling of detachment for a further half-minute—the silent scene had been acted out before me at a distance, encased in glass. It had been like watching television.

The eagles stirred me to my senses. Their cries of distress, the only aural accompaniment to the scene, had not ceased for a moment, and I began to hear them again now. The men below had taken no notice of them either, but now as they had a little time to rest, I could see brown faces and blue chins lift up towards the sky. The shrieks would be associated immediately with the great tree which was as prominent as a statue in a city square. From where they were they would just be able to see a lump wedged beneath the shade of the wide branches. They knew that the area around was stiff with people interfering with the lives of birds, and it was unlikely that they would mistake the object that the eagles jeered at for an unusually athletic lynx. The best that I could hope for was that they were unable to spot from that distance that I had a pair of binoculars. I put them to my eyes again, and saw that Don Sanchez had a pair of his own; large blue-tinged lenses met the Zeiss in a steady gaze that picked out the witness perched high above the scene of activity.

I could not slide down like a brown boy in a coconut tree. I had to go relatively slowly, just as I came up, keeping to the pace of the climbing irons. There was a prickling sensation in my back as I remembered all the equipment Sanchez and his friends were for ever cleaning and polishing or having cleaned and polished. I could recall the telescope attachments on a few of them, though most of the arms were less unsporting. Big calibred guns varying from .280 Rugers to Purdeys to popular express rifles like the semi-automatic two-shot Austrian make which was as expensive as a machine-gun. Dickson 12-bore round-action ejectors; Boss 12-bore sidelock ejectors, Manton 6.bore d.b. hammer rifles. For killing birds or smashing the spines of pigs.

There was no way to hurry down—just a dogged descent, step by step, first over the rough patch, then the smooth stripped bark. The female eagle, seeing me defenceless, moved in as if to give me a sweeping blow. Her wings almost touched my back before she flew off. She came in again and I nearly fell. That would have been the end of it; Jaime would move over so that I could join him in the *cano*. I remembered him that morning, setting off, looking smug as usual.

No, Sanchez could not have a rifle. Rifles, I kept repeating to myself, are forbidden in the reserve. The female eagle shied off triumphantly, having driven me from its territory, and I did the last twenty feet of the descent in a little less of a panic. The group was about three-quarters of a mile away. It was mounted. The leading rider would be up to the tree very soon.

I reached the bottom and pulled off the climbing irons. Only then did I suddenly become conscious of the weight of my binoculars. They had not impeded me in the climb, but now their extra six hundred and eighty grams was an intolerable burden. They were no use to me now, in fact they had been far too useful. But I had time to feel regret as I tore them off my neck and threw them away.

If I could make the scrub, I could conceal myself and gradually veer to my left, back in the direction of the Hafner. Hubert would still be there and perhaps Patterson too. But the eagle's nest was in an isolated tree on a patch of flat sand, and the nearest cover was about three hundred yards away. Even as I picked myself up and started to run, I heard partridge wings giving their curiously mechanical sound. Then the thud of hoofs.

There was no escape by land. I turned and ran down to the edge of the *marismas* and waded in. The water came up above my knees. I attempted to hurry by moving in a high splashing dance, making a lot of noise. My pursuers were still shouting and plunging in the undergrowth, so that they did not hear. But soon they would. I reduced my pace to wading. Here was the classical dream situation, trying to hurry from enemies through treacle.

My gym shoes trod the sticky bottom carefully. Before me stretched sixty-seven thousand acres of muddy brown water, a vast shallow lake dotted with galingale sedge. I had waded about before in the *marismas*, looking for marsh harriers, coots, great reed warblers, purple galinules and such like. I had learned about concealment. To my left and right there were some mixed patches of reedy material, where perhaps I could hide if I made it over the open water. I glided along, smelling the pungent odour of the sedge, willing myself not to splash. Slow steady progress was the only chance. I slung my body from side to side, lifting my feet at each step. If the men came out of the scrub to the edge of the *marismas* now, I would be as conspicuous as the group of cattle I could see in the distance, standing despondently over their truncated reflections.

I got to the first batch of reeds before anyone appeared. Now I had a decision to make. If they continued their search, and guessed I was hiding in the marshes, this location would be the first they would explore. Would I risk moving on another fifty yards through more open water, just as exposed as the distance I had already covered? I hesitated, listening to the distant shouts. They were still in the scrub. I waded on without a glance behind. I was exhausted now. Movement was slow, and my back still twitched in perpetual expectation of a shout of recognition or a bullet. A lot of time passed. But I reached the second batch of reeds.

I felt an exaggerated sense of safety when I managed to conceal myself behind a clump of typha reed-maces. They were over six feet high, and for a few minutes I experienced a security as false as that of a medieval soldier behind a palisade of stakes, waiting for an onslaught of cannon. I peered out through the stout barrier and saw the Moor on horseback standing at the edge of the *marismas*. He might have been there for hours. But he could not have seen me disappear, or he would not be scanning the water, one hand saluting his forehead to keep the sun out of his eyes. There was something medieval-looking about him as well—his scarf tied close round his head, topped with his seedy sombrero made him look like a falconer, especially as the eagles were still flying overhead.

He was joined by the others. Sanchez had brought his binoculars along. You'd think that he, too, would be a customer of Carl Zeiss—but I remembered one of those sessions in the palace drawing room when he had shown off his new American purchase a heavy-weight specialist model boasting some name like Storm King or Audubon. The blue coating on the lenses reduced internal reflections and produced an exceptionally clear image. All the better to see you with, my dear . . . I crouched on all fours behind the reed-maces. My ears were low down and I could hear distant voices skimming over the water.

"He will have doubled back."

"No. He must be hiding out there."

"You can see him with those things?"

"They are powerful, but they cannot look behind reeds. You will have to go out and search. And deal with him."

"As you say."

"I will stay on the bank so that he cannot get back without being seen. Go . . . Javier to the left, Salvador to the right—search every group of reeds. You have your knives?"

I remembered films in which men with good reasons to keep ahead of posses had ended up in swamps. They picked reeds and used them as breathing pipes while they lay submerged. I contemplated yanking out a stretch of reed-mace and lying down. I might as well have tried to pull up the cork tree. Behind me the reeds curved in a sickle and gave way to permanent open water. I could try and wade noisily through them to where ripples and movements would be visible to the binoculars. Or stay where I was and be found by a horseman.

The charcoal burner and the Moor were coming through the water on horseback. The charcoal burner, on Jaime's horse, was going away from me, the Moor approached on a dejected bay whose head he was pulling in several directions. His bridle was made up in the odd Spanish way with two reins, one leading from a snaffle, the second from a nose band. Instead of a saddle the animal appeared to be carrying a lot of old bedding—a folded blanket across its back, over which was perched a pillow backed up by an empty sack. On top was a roughly saddle-shaped piece of felt to which the Moor clung, cursing as he kicked the horse forward. It was a typical horse of the *marismas*, in poor condition, bearing very little resemblance to those

Camargue steeds which appear so frequently on posters and film, tossing their white manes and plunging through foam. Horses on Doñana lack feed most of the year. Although this one was not quite vulture fodder like its wilder brothers, it bore poverty marks, and was not keen on its work. But its progress was steady enough. Soon it had plodded to the first group of reed-maces where I had sought refuge. I could see the Moor peering through the tight natural palisade. Now my own crawling movements would not get me much further ahead. I reached another belt of reeds; beyond it there was only open water peppered with the tops of sedge that would not conceal a mosquito.

Two things saved me. One was the dreadful Spanish caste system. Sanchez might not be an aristocrat by birth, but he had assumed the habits of nobility. Nothing would induce him to leave the bank and join the search, although only his horse's and not his own toes would get wet. He would have been obliged to do the same work as his inferiors. Even when it was a matter of life and death, he preferred to stand there and scream orders, instead of plunging in and helping to flush me out. In few countries west of Bombay is rank considered so important, and pending political change could be justified by that fact alone.

His shouts had the effect of the Moor trying to spur his mount into more lively action. Moving a sluggish horse through sugary brown mud is not an easy task, but he coaxed it into some sort of speed. Then the urgency of his pounding heels communicated the wrong message to the animal and it turned suddenly and slipped. His loud curses made me glance back to glimpse a crouching mud-stained figure trying to pull the horse up to its feet. I took advantage of the agitation to move a little further away, still crawling. But Don Sanchez had not been wasting his time watching his servant's struggles. He was still raking the water with his big binoculars, and I was careless.

"Behind you—further on . . . near that second patch of reed. Javier!"—a shout directed towards the opposite reed bank—"go over and help him." The charcoal burner turned and began to cross the space of water towards his swearing companion who was struggling to remount his horse.

I was well beyond them, but it would not take them long to catch up. In my eagerness to put distance between us, I had

47

moved to open water, and they would soon see my head above the water like a water lily.

The second thing that saved me was the rain that had been threatening all day, for which Jaime had worn his waterproof head covering. It had been preparing itself unnoticed, and now a torrent descended on the surface of the water with a harsh pattering sound that overwhelmed the minor splashes and bumps that were going on round the reeds. Stair rods; I had never before considered what a wonderful simile for rain that was. They blended shutting out images; all the sharp focusing of lenses could not bring me into view as long as the downpour lasted. There was some thunder as well.

I was running in the blessed noisy storm with great skips and leaps. But I could not keep up the pace for more than a few minutes before slowing down to a terrible wading over the puddle that seemed to cover the earth. I looked back; my pursuers were still blotted out behind me. I rested for a few instants before panic moved me on again, panic which could only be translated into a gasping trudge. The Apocalyptic torrent became a handicap more than an instrument of salvation. Then the rain slowed to a cold drizzle that barely pitted the water round my knees. Visibility improved, and I knew now that there was no reason why the people behind should not catch up. The distance could be covered by the horses within minutes. I looked back and made out quite clearly where marsh and scrub met. But I could see no moving figures. I waded on again, an enormous distance, stopping every few seconds to look behind me. Then, after I had gone a mile, maybe a mile and a half, I did not bother to look back any more. I kept on going. I made no attempt to try and change my direction towards the scrub. They might have delayed their pursuit, but they would hardly have given it up. My pace was so much slower than that of their horses.

Later the thunder gave a final growl and the drizzle ceased. The clouds moved over lazily, but they still covered the sun. I looked up and saw a black kite sailing beneath them. I listened, but there was nothing to be heard, and now there was nothing to be seen all round me except water and weed. A little cold breeze started. I stumbled and fell a couple of times, finding myself once more crouching on hands and knees in water. You can drown in three inches, it only needs the nose and mouth to be in the wrong place. I pulled myself up and plunged forward, still wading as fast as I could. Now and again I passed a scrubby bush, adapted to survive inundation in winter and the scorching of summer. I came near to the wild horses and cattle, but never caught up with them. They moved away at my approach, making less splash than I did.

Then I reached the fence. I knew that it divided the boundary of the reserve from privately owned estates. Over the wire was hunting territory; ornithologists might endlessly catch, weigh, ring and release birds, and much of their work would be confirmed by the hunter's gun. (But some birds learned the safety rules and made a point of staying on the right side of the wire.) Eight rusty strands of horizontal barbed wire a foot apart meant that there was no chance of squeezing through; I would either have to climb or make my way along to one of the gates in the fence. And some of those, I knew, were crowned with more wire. Or I could turn back. In those vast spaces, surely I could keep out of sight of three little men?

I climbed. I was shivering, so that my arms got a few nicks from barbs, and it was all that I could do to keep my crotch from being shredded. After the fence the wading got progressively slower. Once a water snake whipped by, bringing me out of a half doze back to reality. My watch had clogged with mud and stopped. It was old, and had never aspired to be proof against the forces of nature. Often it required everything short of the kiss of life to get it going in the morning. Much good it did me now, its hands clasped together at twenty past four. But clouds were arranging themselves round the setting sun, and the sky turned from gold to flamingo. Frogs started up as the odd bird drifted by to roost.

As it grew dark my thoughts were possessed by cold more than panic. I recalled a passage from Abel Chapman when he described camping in the *marismas* during what he chose to call his "campaigns in winter". "One is waked in the middle watches of the night by the sheer penetrating cold, finds the fire burnt out, the trusted Espanoles asleep and the tail of a big snake sticking out from under the bed . . ." At least Chapman was on dry land and could kick the fire and the trusted Espanoles awake.

There was a light ahead, a green tinged glow like a will of the wisp. Could I have waded all the way across the *marismas*

49

already? That would be a distance of six or eight miles. Then I remembered that people still lived in the heart of the marshes. There is perpetual talk in Spain of housing shortages and families having to put up with caves and cellars. Here in Andalusia some make their homes like herons. They endure one of the most uncomfortable and isolated lifestyles in Europe in reed houses perched on high ground above the marshes. In winter the land around them is covered in water so that they are confined to diminishing islands. Often these are flooded. Only in summer, when the water dries up and the ground becomes dried and parched do these *chozas* have direct communication with the rest of Spain.

The black rectangle of the *choza* in front of me was outlined like a haystack against the stars. There were no windows in the reed walls, but the door which extended from floor to ceiling was open, and the light came from the interior, wandering outside for a small space, lapping a couple of constructions that might have been hen runs or tool sheds.

As I waded out of the water on to the dry land, a dog began barking. It did not come outside to threaten or discourage me, but remained somewhere in the interior, its voice echoing. When I went up to the big door and stepped inside, it was at my feet at once, a black dog, snapping and growling. There was no other movement. I stood in the one room that ran the full length of the hut. It was in chaos, and the squalor revealed by the cool lemon light of a gas lamp, seemed to be emphasized by the jungle atmosphere imparted by the reed walls and high pitched, neatly thatched roof. The reeds, layered near the bottom in frills like a flamenco dancer's skirt, pressed in on the filthy crockery and unwashed saucepans; the smells of bad food, sour wine, olive oil, urine and vomit were not dissipated by the cold air coming through the open door. Bottles were everywhere, green bottles mostly, that covered part of the floor like fungus and clustered around the hissing lamp on the deal table. A lot of liquid had spilt and seeped into the mud of the floor, making dark stains. On one reed wall were tacked photographs of vintage cars and a local bullfighter, Jose Luis Pareda. Over to the left with space to herself was an outsize postcard, framed in *passe-partout*, showing one of Seville's most venerated Virgins, La Macarena, with glass tears stuck on to her wooden cheeks. The place seemed empty of human life, as if whoever had caused the mess could not stand it any more and had stumped off into the marshes. The lamp gave a faint hiss, drowned most of the time by the dog's hysterical orchestration. There was a little heat from it which suggested recent human presence. I might be coming aboard the *Mary Celeste*. The room was big and high, and full of dark corners unreached by the gas light, so that it took me some time to notice the stirring heap of rags and sacks with a line of bottles arranged beside it like a palisade. An arm and then another lifted into the air, waving like seaweed fronds, and the man sat up.

"*Que tal, Caesar?*" Everywhere the Roman empire flourished people call their dogs Caesar. His voice had the same note as the frogs I had heard at dusk. "I am here!" I called out tentatively, and he looked round the place for about half a minute before locating me beside the deal table. He got up quickly with hardly a stagger, and crossed himself. Then he side-stepped and reached down to pick up the nearest thing to hand. An axe. I felt a twinge of regret that I had ever taken up stealing birds' eggs. The D.T.'s affect people differently. He was running round the table now, waving the axe and shouting, taking no notice of my cries of help and mercy. I should have run outside—possibly I had a subconscious preference for the side of his axe to a return to the cold marsh water, where I could have escaped him easily enough. But I also felt a stirring of rage. "My mind went blank", a lot of murderers say about the moment of their crime. But mine didn't; I was motivated by fear, coupled with an enlarged sense of grievance. It was wholly unfair that after escaping the threat of death from three strangers I should be driven within range of this furious drunkard. I had weapons of defence ranged in front of me. I picked up a bottle and threw it. It missed and landed silently in his withered bedding. I seized a second and hurled it with all my strength. It fell unbroken on to the floor. A third smashed into the picture of a Mercedes Benz, circa 1904. I grabbed a fourth. "Stop ... Listen ... No ..." How had he got me away from the table into the far corner from the door? He carried the axe in both hands now, and was waving it as he ran forward. I hurled the bottle I was carrying with all my strength. It also fell unbroken on to the floor, but on the way it stove in his temple with a pulpy sound.

When I looked at him properly I saw that he was an old fellow, red-faced and dressed in the short jacket and trousers that was the general uniform worn by guards and foresters. I didn't recognize him; he was not one of those who frequented the palace. Like Jaime he had a white mark on his forehead where his hat had shaded him for a lifetime, only some of the white was now covered with the purple bruising that spread around that smashed side of his face. He was more unshaven than any man I saw that day; the grey stubble had become a pelt that caressed his cheek. His eyes were open but I could not make out much of them. The pupils were turned up from the bloodshot spaces of his whites, into the top of his head, so that only two little brown half circles were visible beneath his eyelids.

Turning my attention back to the bottles lined up on the deal table, I found, after a long search, one that was about a quarter full of rough brandy. I carried it over to the grease-stained deckchair which was the only place he had for relaxation apart from his horrible bed. I slumped down and drank a couple of big mouthfuls. In front of me the dog was whining non-stop. It had crawled along the floor on its stomach until it reached its master's corpse, where it planted the underside of its jaw on his knee.

I took another swallow and glanced down to see that I too, had been wounded. Blood poured out of one sleeve. And the other. I looked down and more blood emerged from beneath my trouser legs. I got up and tore off my clothes. I was streaming like an Easter week statue. Leeches hung off my body like mournful Christmas tree ornaments. Cigarettes would get them off. My own were in the bag I had abandoned near the binoculars beneath the cork tree. The man I had killed smoked; I found stubs crushed out in the oil of an empty sardine tin. But he had run out—the two Duocados packets thrown on the kitchen table were empty. Salt was the other remedy for leeches. After another search among crumbs and mouse droppings I found some in a thick brown paper packet. I grabbed handfuls and rubbed them against the black slug-like creatures, which curled and dropped off reluctantly. There were dozens, all over my legs and up to my waist. After they had come off I looked as if it had been a Chinaman who had started killing me, using the death of a thousand cuts and giving up in boredom before he got halfway.

And just before laying down his knife he made a zig-zag movement where the eagle's talon had scored me. That was the only wound that hurt. But the others would continue to bleed, because leeches use an anti-coagulant to assist them at mealtimes. I felt cold. I considered remaining naked for a time, wrapping myself in some of the dead man's bedding. The idea revolted me, and eventually, still bleeding, I dressed again. The trousers were sodden, but they would soon become wet again in any case. I slumped down in the deckchair and had some more brandy.

The air was full of small noises—the hum of mosquitoes that had come winging in through the door, the steady hiss of the lamp and the small unhappy sounds made by the dog. I had not bothered to cover up the dead man, and I could see part of his face, like something painted by Francis Bacon. His hand showed as well, the fingers stretched out very wide as if he were measuring. My God, I had killed him. Murdered him. He had nothing to do with Don Sanchez. Nothing in common except a tendency to violence. There were some rusty traps heaped in a corner and an old shot-gun. I took him to be a retired guard or gamekeeper, drinking himself to a solitary death. I had hastened on the process.

I got up and walked stiffly over to the debris with which I was becoming familiar. I had spotted half a loaf of dark bread there, together with a couple of *chorizos*. They tasted good. There was water in a tin bucket—he may not have drunk it often, but I took a deep draught now. I searched in a box of nails and odds and ends and came up with a needle attached to some pack thread. I took the box out of my anorak and opened it. The egg was intact. I pierced both ends and blew it.

I could do the same thing with the dead man as they had done to Jaime. Hide him. Then I would make my way back to the palace and leave. Leave Doñana, leave Spain before any questions were asked.

My man would turn up again in due course. Jaime was safe and sound in his *cano*. This one I could only dump somewhere in the water outside his cottage and hope that the sedge would grow around him before he was discovered. It would become luxuriant and remain so for about six weeks. If no one found him he would be shrouded in it until the sun finally soaked up the last of the marsh water. By that time he would have been exposed to various scavengers. Before very long he would become bones, one of the thousands of skeletons of deer, cattle, horses and untold numbers of birds who died when the hot weather came. Where does a wise man hide a leaf? In a forest. I began to feel quite sorry for Don Sanchez. He had bad luck in finding a witness at the one spot of all lonely Doñana where he was trying to solve his disposal problem.

When I put my man over my shoulder and waded into the marsh outside his front door, his weight made me sink deep into the mud. I had to pull up each foot each time I took a step. I did not carry him very far before I stopped and heaved him ahead of me into the water. I couldn't see if he disappeared. I really should have tried harder to get him to stay down. He would be floating soon and it would be some time before the sedge grew big enough to conceal him. Before that anyone who came to the *choza* might spot him. But there was no need for suspicion to fall on me; tomorrow I might give a convincing enough story about staying out all night to count nightjars. Something like that. And then leave the country. I would think it out later. I was hurrying now.

I went back inside the *choza* and wiped as many surfaces free of fingerprints as I remembered having touched. I picked up the bottle that had killed him off the floor. It was a litre container of tough bluish glass that required stone or brick to break it—not packed sand or the tender bones on a man's forehead. The old-fashioned spring and rubber top was of a kind that has become antique in England. I sniffed inside and caught a whiff of sulphur. Some kind of mineral water. The label said REVOLTOSA which I took to mean something like *Bubbly*. *Bebida Refrescante,* it continued, *Elaborada con Agua Tratada Bacteriologicalmente.* It was the only bottle that I could see that didn't contain alcohol. Temperance people might like to make something of that.

I took a final look round. The number of bottles was quite staggering. In one corner beside the filthy little burner on which he cooked were several wooden boxes full of empties. They must have been carried here full with some effort and labour. There was a lot of other debris—ropes, nails, a few things like that, a lot of stinking clothes and rags, some empty gas bombs that had been used for the light and stove, and a cardboard box containing one unused spare. And there was the dog.

I didn't know what to do about the dog. I knew it would be kinder to destroy it in some way, and as I handled *Revoltosa* I thought about ways and means. There was the axe. Also his old shot-gun. No cartridges as far as I could see, although I did nose about in the boxes full of oddments. Everything I touched I wiped clean. I felt rather badly, but in the end I left the dog trembling and whining, creeping about the floor on its belly, the very incarnation of Churchill's synonym for depression.

The temperature of the water was lowered to a degree that made my legs numb. I looked back once towards the *choza* and its light. The sky was turning grey and then lightening as the stars vanished. Soon I was once more shipwrecked in a shallow sea. I plodded on, hating the marshes, hating the small herd of fallow deer which came into my vision proudly waving flattened antlers. I hated the birds, too, that I kept glimpsing. So short a time before I had rejoiced that they lived in the *marismas* for my delight.

I decided not to recross the wire and return directly to the palace. I was still afraid that Don Sanchez and his men might be waiting anywhere, and even if they were not, I did not want to draw suspicion on to myself. When the dead man at the *choza* was found any eccentric behaviour on my part would be remembered. Before that, if I got clear of the country, I might disassociate myself from the whole episode. Two dead men. Get out before the bodies were found. I had killed one. Suppose I did report what I had seen, as I should, instead of letting a group of murderers go free? Better not. Better for me. I didn't want anything to do with it.

I had studied many maps of Doñana. The *choza* behind me must be located somewhere in the area of the Marismas de Alcanar, a large area of reed and water bordered by two other shallow seas—the so-called Junta de los Canos to the north and the Lucio de Maria Lopez to the south. If I wanted to get out of the water, I could either turn back towards the palace—which I had already decided not to do—or continue eastward towards the newly established rice fields on the Isla Major. That was the way. Before I got to them I would have to cross the Brazo de la Torre, a tributary of the Guadalquivir. But beyond that

I would find towns. Villafranco was the nearest and the largest. I would go to Villafranco and hire some sort of transport to take me back to the palace. I had money in my anorak; I always carried some on egg-hunting expeditions, ever since I had been able to pay off a gamekeeper employed by a Scottish Marquis who found me after a golden eagle's nest. I would go back to the palace openly, pretending perhaps that I had stayed away for the night at Juan de la Frontera or one of the coastal resorts. No, hardly that in my filthy condition. Perhaps I might pretend to be ill? There was flu about; some of the kitchen staff had it. I could come in, faintly delirious with that unlikely story about watching night birds. Discourage questions and doctors and retire to bed. And in a day or two I would leave Doñana.

I tried to put my mind to the series of actions played out by four figures within the rounded stage of my binocular lenses. What had they been doing? One of the actors was an important Andalusian businessman and landowner. Had Jaime's death involved smuggling? Politics? Foreigners tend to believe that all acts of violence in Spain, with a few exceptions like the climax of Carmen, occur in the bull ring or are politically motivated. The average scientist at the palace felt roughly the same interest in Spain's political reawakening as the package tourist did. And in some respects I was an average scientist. I had only been curious about possible political change insofar as it affected bird counts. Wars and civil disturbances used to be rather good for birds, who got ignored when there was no time or leisure to hunt them. Who had said something like that recently? Patterson? But nothing is safe in modern warfare, and birds can become casualties of napalm or of defoliation programmes, same as everything else.

Why assume Jaime's death was politically motivated any more than the incident at the *choza* which, I kept telling myself, had been a matter of self defence. I hoped I had wiped away all traces of myself. Every fingerprint. I hoped that when that dead man was found, even if the authorities suspected my involvement, there would not be enough evidence to call me back to Spain. It all depended if I had cleaned up properly or not.

The winter would not be entirely wasted. I had enough notes on Abel Chapman for a book and a film. The film could start with shots of stuffed birds—all the species he had shot. Most of them would be on display in the Natural History Museum in London. Alternated with views of the same birds alive. Great bustards, herons, flamingoes, imperial eagles, of course. Rifle sounds. A bearded actor, such as the BBC used when it did that series on explorers. Later, if I ever got out of this marsh, I would go somewhere where birds were completely different. South America perhaps. For a long time as I waded I thought about condors and hoatzin.

The sun rose and got smaller. Far ahead I could see the faint frieze of the Sierra de San Cristobal looming beyond the Guadalquivir plain. I even thought I could make out a village—a crown of white houses on a hill, topped by a church tower. There would be a stork's nest on it, and underneath houses staggered beside cobbled alleys, falling precipitously to the fields. Housewives sitting tethered to doorways—the animation of the small town restrained by the angle at which the inhabitants lived. Most of the shops and all the bars would be further down on a less acute slope: society as symmetrical as on the Hill of Purgatory. I had been wading for hours and my legs were weak and papery. Thinking of the bustle of cafés with their invitation to eat, I felt a renewed surge of self pity.

Suddenly I realized with exquisite relief that I was not condemned to stay in the water for ever. I had caught sight of a shimmering line ahead of me. I knew that this was one of the ecological barriers that marked off the limits of the *marismas*, and soon I could identify it as reed-mace flanking the sluggish muddy brown stream of the Brazo de la Torre. Once this must have been a considerable river, but now its water was drained away for irrigating the new rice fields. The *marismas* came to an abrupt end just where the river had been lowered and deepened. Its new high banks were constructed out of mud dredged from its own bed; they had been straightened out so that its natural route was marshalled into what was more or less a canal. On the far side the rice fields began.

I was looking at direct evidence of how the area which made such an ideal habitat for wild life was being reduced. The reed-mace was the last outpost for the birds. And they knew it. Most of them kept to the *marismas* side of the river, and the reeds bustled with cattle egrets, lapwings and little stints. I even glimpsed a Bonelli eagle well this side of the rice fields.

57

But now I did not care about conservation. The whole dreary stretch of water could be drained for rice in an instant for all that I cared. The prospect of civilization seemed infinitely inviting, and I was not worried about the reduction of the birds' playground. I had other preoccupations. I had to cross the river. The distance to the far bank had to be swum, and the water was foul and cold. Because of the current I was carried down quite a long way before I made it to the other side. Later I lay down on the far bank, smelling the mud on my clothes. I checked up on the egg I carried in my pocket; the little white case had held it safe. I took out the squelching stinking roll of pesetas and spread them carefully on my chest. The sun was already beginning to dry my clothes and my money as I fell asleep.

Chapter four

THE STINK IN my clothes was less conspicuous—at least until I sat up and realized that my back still retained intimations of the marshes. I was like a cowpat, sundried on top, mucky underneath. The peseta notes, curled up and dried in queer positions like men who had died on a battlefield, were just recognizable as money.

On the whole, considering the last few hours, I wasn't in too bad a condition. I checked up on leeches, and curiously enough found only two. The density of leeches varies in different parts of the *marismas*; some leech-eating birds flourish where there are large quantities. The distribution is perhaps related to salinity. I had no salt or ash to remove them, but the thought of carrying these unpleasant passengers nauseated me. I did the wrong thing, and tore them off my ankles, leaving a couple of weeping wounds.

Thirst nagged me so that I contemplated the patches of water appearing through the reeds in the ditch beside me. Still water, in which bacteria was almost visible. Although I had ceased to be fastidious, I discarded the idea of lying down and sucking up a drink like one of Gideon's thirsty route marchers. Hunger was less of a torment. I would wait; a town could not be too far away.

I set off along one of the numerous tracks that stretched across the rice fields. The rice spread around me over territory which until recently consisted of a reedy island called Isla Major, surrounded by *marismas*. The scrub and marsh had created the usual Doñana environment where birds, wild horses, deer and wild boar had flourished. Miles of silvery water in winter and scorched flats in summer had separated the Isla from the nearest town. But now a lot of it had been soaked up, and in its place was one of the richest agricultural areas in Spain. Fertile delta land was divided by banks of earth and canals which controlled the flooding of the fields. The process of reducing the marsh area was continuing, and I could see evidence of new drainage schemes. Coils of yellow pipes lay where new ditches had been dug. Foundations of new farms and pumping stations were visible. Spain and the world needed rice; birds were a luxury. A solitary kite hovered above the tamed landscape; a few egrets lingered on the rice beds.

Streamers of light pierced the grey sky, picking out details of the surrounding plain—a small farmhouse with its apron for drying rice, the flash of a metal storage bin, the even patterns of rice fields stretching to the horizon. I noticed plumes of smoke thrown up against the sky above the outline of factory chimneys smudged against the green rice shoots. A factory meant a town.

Out of the tracks that formed a grid over the fields I chose one that followed a canal in the direction of the chimneys. It was a dismal route, marked by heaps of rubbish, old tins and the flattened shapes of snakes and other reptiles that had been run over by tractors and lorries. I came to a pumping station which flooded water into the paddies, and lingered outside it for some time, wondering if I would knock up whoever was within and ask for a drink of *agua*. When I finally screwed up courage and hammered at the door, I found that the place was shut up and deserted. Distributing water into the paddies was only an intermittent process. Later I came to a straw hut with a rusted sign for Coca Cola and a heap of garbage beside it. Ahead of me, far away, a dark shape suddenly became larger. A lorry. I preferred to merge into the filth beside the hut and the vehicle roared by without a pause. But a mile further on, when the track was quite empty except for the odd mangled frog, a Yamaha suddenly came buzzing towards me, having turned sharply out of yet another track in the grid. Reasoning that I would make myself more conspicuous if I tried to hide in the ditch beside me, I kept walking firmly. Perhaps if he had been on a bicycle he might have stopped and stared and passed the time of day. But rice fields brought prosperity—enough for him to buy his scooter. A dark man in a beret, he passed me without a glance.

A wind had sprung up, smothering the plain in particles of dust. The first houses appeared out of nowhere and the great bulk of the factory. Two large chimneys grew out of a corrugated shed filled with the hiss of steam pipes and the rumble of machinery. I peered into the yard where bales of rice straw were waiting to be turned into paper. A siren was blowing and men in overalls were streaming out of doors. With a start I realized that I must have slept and walked away most of the day, and now it was evening again. I glanced around; yes, the sun was low on the horizon behind some eucalyptus trees.

I joined the stream of workmen going home, mostly on scooters, a few on bicycles and a fair sprinkling of pedestrians making their way towards a bridge with a signpost beside it. VILLA-FRANCO DEL GUADALQUIVIR. POBLADO QUIPO DE LALLANO. Now I remembered the name. Villafranco was a new town which represented the triumph of civilization over Doñana. Once I visited the plains in central Italy that had formed part of the Pontine marshes; Mussolini drained them, bringing new agriculture and destroying the bird life way back in 1935. Here in Spain was another district with similar origins, marshland drained under Fascist regimes. Although Isla Major was thirty years younger than the Pontine area, its towns had precisely the same atmosphere of instant shabbiness. The superficial smartness of the Farnese style gets washed away in one winter's rain. Villafranco had a long main street made up of machine shops, concrete flats, bars, and the factories. Architectural effort was limited and aesthetics were represented by some avenues of eucalyptus trees and a little park with a statue, Libertad or something, or maybe a virgin overseeing a war memorial.

Decisions, decisions. First of all I was thirsty. My tongue was swollen and dry, with the texture and taste of a large old tea bag. I went into the most crowded bar I could see, which was called Bar Isla. Television dominated it. The men round the counter were watching Kojak suck a lollipop prior to beating up someone who leaned against a wall. The colour was not adjusted properly, and the brilliant screen looked as if it had been painted by Van Gogh.

Cerveza? The barman could do better than produce the local stuff. He had some tall cold bottles of Pilsen. Blessing the local prosperity, I drank off one straight away, and then asked for a second, which I sipped more slowly. Kojak was coming to an end; the man against the wall turned out to be the most horrible villain. People's attention lapsed as the programme changed and the news came on. The announcer's face was orange, his tie sunset pink. He showed the King and Queen of Spain in panto-mime clothes, attending an official function. A brief shot of a crowd in a Basque town in a frame of mounted police. The latest economic worries of Great Britain were relayed in tones of satisfaction.

There was my passport photograph in stark black and white, a contrast to the announcer's bright complexion. It stared out of the screen with an air of youth and surprise. Coming from a document that had survived years of travel and renewal, it seemed a study of schoolboy innocence. When I passed through frontiers, officials had to examine it carefully before they made the connection between the small square likeness taken in the Edgware Road nine years ago and the reality. I had married, fathered a son and been divorced since the photographer perpetuated that stiffened leer.

The announcer was saying that the body of a man who met his death by violent means had been discovered beside the *marismas* in the *Estación Biologica* of the Coto Doñana. He had been identified as Dr Dougal McNair Patterson, a distinguished English ornithologist, who had been studying birds at the *Estación*.

Patterson would have hated being described as English, was my first thought. A conversational theme of his had been Scottish or was it Scotch national aspirations.

The *guardia civil* of the El Rocio district were searching for another English ornithologist who was suspected of having perpetrated the crime. Nothing so subtle as helping with enquiries. Robert Ingalls O'Donnell Lacey—the names were reeled off from the passport. He was known to have had several disagreements with Doctor Patterson. I was a doctor too, but seemed to have lost my status. He had been in the area where the body was discovered at approximately the time of the murder.

I swivelled my eyes from left to right. No one appeared to be listening. News was nearly always uninteresting, and even this local sensation failed to raise more than a few glances at the screen. Perhaps censorship had battered the truth too long for people to take notice even of local events. The crime concerned foreigners. Interest in broadcasting was only resumed when football came on and a player kicked a goal and was kissed by his friends.

I left hastily, pushing through the crowd, opening the glass door and stepping outside. The *paseo* was in full swing. Aimless couples, groups of girls, family parties, jeering young men, paraded up and down. I slipped into the Jacob's ladder procession.

I knew now why Don Sanchez and his men had not pursued me and murdered me. The easy way that I had lost them in the rain was illusory. In fact they *had* followed and killed the man they assumed to be me.

Patterson must have trailed me. He may have told Hubert of his suspicions, if the motive of our disagreement had become public so quickly. Ostensibly Patterson and I had merely disliked each other. Hubert had probably refused to believe the story that I was an egg thief, and stuck to his watch at the Hafner, while Patterson assumed his self-appointed task of following me. He had come along quietly, just as I had feared he would, caring as little for the welfare of imperial eagles as I did. Otherwise surely he could have prevented me from taking one more small step towards their extermination. No, he wished to catch me in the act. I had underestimated his skill; years of stalking shy birds helped him to sneak after me without my catching a glimpse of him during my nervous searchings through the Zeiss from up the cork tree. He had continued his advance while I was watching the scene at the *cano*. And then, too late, he had emerged beside the *marismas* in the pouring rain.

Sanchez had assumed that I was hiding in the water, presumably after catching a glimpse of me through his own powerful binoculars. An inconclusive glimpse, but enough to make him imperiously order his servants to wade out into the water in search of me. He must have felt a loss of face when he turned and saw a man striding out of the scrub. Patterson and I had a similar build and colouring and we wore equally nondescript clothes. And we both carried binoculars. Sanchez must have forgotten for a moment that in that area men with binoculars were as common as magpies. Never mind; Patterson was killed quickly in mistake for me.

Why wasn't he lying in the *cano* beside Jaime with a stone around his feet? There may not have been time to dump him. Or it may have simply been better to leave him to be discovered. Jaime's murder had been carefully concealed. Now with Patterson dead. Sanchez had acquired a reason for Jaime's disappearance. When they examined Patterson's body the intelligent authorities would assume that Jaime had killed him and fled.

But things had not turned out like that. The body had been

found very quickly ... perhaps Hubert had finally wandered down from the Hafner. There were known to be disagreements between Patterson and me. My binoculars, bag and climbing irons would have been discovered near the cork tree and the eagle's nest. It would naturally be assumed that I had killed him.

But Sanchez would realize that I was still alive. A witness to Jaime's elaborate concealment. He and his associates might retrieve his body out of the *cano* and bury it elsewhere. But they would also be searching for me again. To kill me if possible. I was a continual danger to them, whether I was at liberty or in the leisurely confines of a Spanish prison.

All I had to do was to go down one of Villafranco's dismal streets to the police barracks and tell my story. And also explain about the man I had killed in the *marismas*.

I went as far as identifying the long white building which was large enough to hold a garrison. There was a group of *guardia* outside it and more mingled with the *paseo*. I had experienced the usual dealings of foreigners with *guardia civil* in rural places—the careful scrutiny of the passport, the suggestion that it might be better to move on. None of the local antagonisms rising from harsh loyalties and cruel memories. But now I must convince them in my fluent kitchen Spanish that I had seen Don Sanchez oversee a *vaquero*'s burial. Why would he want to do a thing like that? You yourself could have put the body in the *cano* just as easily, señor. And then he had murdered or supervised the murder of Dr Patterson? Your enemy? You yourself had a far better motive for killing the doctor than the eminent Don Sanchez— landowner, employer, patron, hotel owner. And then there is the case of the lonely defenceless old man whom you actually admit killing.

One could remain in a Spanish prison for years. Like being preserved on ice. Never be persuaded that foreigners are unnecessarily alarmed about Spanish law. It's true that those who bring in foreign currency and whose transgressions aren't too serious usually receive favourable treatment. You have your green card, international car insurance? Then if you are involved in a car accident, of course, you can get bail. Unless, of course, the circumstances indicate criminal negligence. But what about other crimes? What about the law's delays?

Strange that I should know about Spanish law. Lightning

striking twice in the same family. Poor Michael's troubles had taken place more than five years ago. He had attempted to smuggle hash from Morocco across Spain. He and his car and his friends were picked up near Malaga. After that we learned all about the Spanish legal system. Founded on the French, which meant that a *magistrat d'instruction* is appointed in criminal cases. His job is to prepare a dossier which becomes the basis for both defence and prosecution cases. Of course, often he is a busy man, and it might take him some time before the case is ready to come up for trial. Two years? It could even be three or four.

I remembered the fate of Michael's friend. The one who had organized the whole trip from Morocco. A Madrileño whose family was well connected. It may have been a coincidence, but he had been released remarkably quickly after his arrest. Lack of evidence. I wondered if he had been better connected than Don Sanchez. Michael had been left to carry the can. He had not survived prison conditions; he was asthmatic. He died unnoticed, except for a couple of lines in Irish newspapers—Cork man dies in Spanish jail. Eighteen months and his case was still in the hands of the magistrate.

Michael's troubles might have been exceptional. Like me he had been guilty—up to a point. I did not think that my case would improve like old Amontillado if it was kept waiting for eighteen months. There was a dead man in the *marismas* whose death could only be ascribed to me. Sooner or later he would have to be accounted for.

Well, what else could I do? Try and escape out of the country? To Gibraltar where I could make my explanations under a Union Jack? Or go down to Torremolinos and mingle with the package tours? Steal a passport and return on a chartered aeroplane? My position was not one to invite international sympathy. If—when —I was arrested, I would have the same sad-clown status of all foreigners who get involved in crimes, petty and serious, outside their own countries and find themselves trapped in distant jails. I was not a figure of dignity. A petty thief turned murderer. An ecological outcast.

Joaquín. Don Joaquín, rather. Another bloody Don. Probably remote and ineffectual. But it might be helpful if I could consult someone neutral before the Spanish police got hold of me. I had first come across him in Teneriffe where his family owned a luxurious villa. He had been interested in mountaineering and rock climbing, and had helped me in my search for swift colonies. A lawyer, whose opinions had been too liberal for him to prosper during the last long regime, although they had always seemed to me to be well to the right of—say—Mrs Thatcher's. He had a voice in the new national setup struggling not to jail too many socialists. A friend of mine if I still had friends. I would be a nasty embarrassment when I arrived at the door of his office and asked him to ease my way through the Spanish legal system. There was just a faint chance that he might help me. Unlike my naturalist colleagues, he wouldn't automatically believe me a villain because I stole birds' eggs. He was the sort of person who might have access to unlikely information about Don Sanchez and suggest a motive for his actions. He might arrange means whereby my story could be investigated independently. He would be a good ally to recruit—and once I was in jail I would find it much more difficult to contact him.

It was a thin pretext for keeping away from the police barracks.

Joaquín practised in Seville.

Villafranco was no place to stay. A foreigner couldn't remain unrecognized here. Of course foreigners were to be found in most places. Old English couples, retired American airforce officials, German nymphomaniacs, tourists and estate agents of every nationality had become as much a part of the Andalusian scene as the gypsy and the muleteer. But there would not be many among the flat rice fields of the Isla Major.

I would go to Seville. I didn't worry about Sanchez and the danger from his pursuit. That was associated with the *marismas* and I was out of there now. Out of his territory. Stupidly I hardly gave him a thought. I was more concerned with getting out of Villafranco. I found the bus station and saw from a notice that the one daily bus to Seville left at seven next morning. I would have to spend a night here. Not in a hotel, even if there was such a thing here. I thought fleetingly about a prison cell. I would eat first.

More prosperity was evident in the brightly lit shop windows. In addition to colour television sets and bottled gas cookers, there were luxuries like Chinese mandarins holding up lamps, plastic

African heads, chromium-plated beds, coffee tables whose legs ended in gold paws, virgins, holy infants and blood-splashed figures of saints. Among the shops were the bars and cakeshops. I studied menus—*pescado planchas, langostinos planchas, filete de cerdo, corqueta por espada*; through a restaurant window I watched men settling down to plates of butterfly coloured seafood. But a restaurant would be risky. The waiter talks, you talk, he looks into your eyes. If I wanted to eat, it would have to be with another group of distracted people.

In the Bar Doñana more men were watching more television. Andalusian gaiety, I thought, is as much a myth as Irish laughter. *Tapas* were laid out on the bar counter, and I was soon stuffing myself with shrimps, peeling and sucking them noisily, scattering shells round my ankles. They were fussy things to satisfy hunger on, but the little biscuits in saucers beside them helped, and so did a bottle of wine.

This time I was noticed. As I became overconfident with each glass that I drank, I failed to see that some of those beside me or behind me were not engrossed in the serial about being lost in space. The men who spotted me must either have known me by sight or linked the televised mug shot with a glimpse of my bottleframed face in the bar mirror. I had time to study it myself while I nibbled shrimps. The red-eyed unshaved image that glowered behind Coca Cola's sloping scarlet italics did not have much resemblance to the young man portrayed above my passport signature. But someone made the connection.

I did not hear them or sense they were behind me when I walked down the main street. There were fewer people about now, and apart from the nocturnal rumble of factory machinery, the most dominant sound in Villafranco was the tinny chatter of starlings settling down in a group of palms. The pavement was lit with carbide lamps. I passed the last shop window which showed a faded photograph of a fat young man with the caption QUIEN ES GURU MAHARAJ JI.

Another factory. Large sheds round a dark yard where the gentle noise of machines ticking over for the night could be identified more precisely. I went around without hesitation, not thinking about the possibility of guard dogs. Everything locked and bolted except for one door leading into a wooden extension to the main building from where a light shone through a window and Spain's golden pop singer, Julio Iglesias, was bellowing out a song called *A flor de piel*. A transistor. I sidled up to the window and peered in. An old man was reading a paper. There were crutches by his chair, and I saw that he had lost a leg. I guessed that he might be a war veteran rewarded with a comfortable job as caretaker.

He looked comfortable. This was the wrong place for me to be, everything locked and the night cold. The alternative seemed rice fields or the guards' barracks. As I hesitated before deciding to make my way back towards the town, there was a movement in the lighted office and the next moment some lights came on in the yard. The caretaker had limped over to a switch-board. Dim lights, faint bulbs under enamel shades.

His round of the factory could be little more than a courtesy tour, like beef-eaters taking their pikes round the Tower of London. As he limped slowly down the steps from his office, I could see his face under the yard light which accentuated the plateresque detail of his wrinkles. Leaning on his crutches, he made his way across the yard.

I was longing for shelter. The open door at the top of the steps down which he had just made his way offered an opportunity for me to get out of the wind. It seemed to link up with a part of the main factory building, and as the caretaker's disabilities so obviously slowed him down, I took the risk, ran up and slipped inside. My surmise was correct; at the far end of the wooden hut an unlocked door led into a sparsely lit passage flanked by other doors. The current singer on the transistor was chortling a cheerful ballad about *Lady Marmalade*. I tried the first two doors, which were locked; the third pushed open into a cloakroom. Basins, lavatories, a line of wooden lockers, and, better still, boiler suits hanging on hooks. They seemed to come in two sizes, large and small with a preponderance of small. I selected a large one, and taking it down, transferred my money and the eagle's egg from the pocket of my anorak to the pocket of my new acquisition. I stripped off all my old clothes which had become so saturated with dried mud that I could not fold them without releasing clouds of brown dust. I threw them up on to the top of the lockers before climbing into the boiler suit, which just fitted, hugging me so tightly that it might better have been described as a lagging jacket. I examined myself in a long mirror before which endless men must have done up their flies, adjusted their collars and combed back their rich dark hair. I thought I made a passable Spanish workman. The signs of fatigue that had appeared so horrific in the bar mirror now merely mimicked the haggard expression of any Spaniard with an uncertain job and a large family. I even had a midweek growth of beard.

Out of the cloakroom the other doors in the passage were locked. But there was a staircase, and the door with glass panels at the top was half open. I went up and through it into a large hall, where I found myself standing at the beginning of a wooden catwalk high up almost under the roof. Windows above me tipped open or shut with ropes. The catwalk encircled a space in the centre as large as a squash court, which was covered with a flattened, slightly undulating heap of husked rice. Little highlights gleamed on the surface, picked out by the flourescent bulbs that hung from the ceiling. A chain fence, waist high, edged the catwalk and prevented people from falling off. On the far side there was a small gate in the fence, through which anyone could reach the plain of rice below. So much was stored here at the moment that it was just a little step out of the gate on to the great mass that covered the floor. I assumed that at other times much of the amount would be cleared away and sold or exported or whatever they did with it, and then the gate would merely give way on to a drop to the ground below. The fourth wall of the hall was mostly taken up by two vast double doors that would be opened in daytime, allowing supplies to come in and out. All the action was down there; the wooden passage up here must be used for adjusting ventilation, perhaps for measuring quantities or taking samples. I circled the catwalk and found that the door at the far end leading out of the storage hall was locked. I would have to go back. In front of it I found a pile of sacks and a spade. It seemed a feeble way of reducing the mound in the middle. There must be mechanical methods of parcelling up and distributing the product. More likely, way up here, very nearly out of sight, someone was helping himself. A half-dozen sackfuls taken at regular intervals that would never be missed. Perhaps it was the caretaker who considered them his perks? As I stood contemplating them the lights went out overhead. He had finished his round and turned them off at the switchboard without even coming and checking up the storage hall.

I didn't like the idea of creeping back in the darkness, down the steps and trying to make my way past the old man. And then what? A night spent among the flooded paddies or in the town? A firm decision to give myself up? Either involved an initial conversation with the caretaker, now doubtless back in his office. He might well be armed. Surely no one that decrepit could be in such a position without something to reinforce him? I began groping about trying to make up a rough bed of sacks. There weren't anywhere near enough. Then I thought I might be more comfortable if I actually lay on top of the rice; it would be soft and insulated better than the hard rickety floor of the catwalk. By this time I could see something of my surroundings as my eyes picked out the white surface of the rice grains reflecting a little light from the night sky outside the windows. I could see where the gate was in the fence a few yards away, and when I went up to it, I found that it was held shut with a bolt. I opened it and lowered myself on to the spreading plain of rice. I felt a slight crust resist my feet for a second and then give way as I realized that I had been a fool. I broke into a sweat. Only by luck did I still have my arms resting on the rough wooden edge of the catwalk. Otherwise I would have slid smoothly down into ten or twelve feet of yielding grain.

Shuddering I heaved myself out, shut the bolt hastily, and went over to the sacks where I sat down aching with weariness and a growing knowledge of a bleak lifetime stretching ahead of me. And before that happened I longed for a warm bed with the avidness of a drowning man seeking a foothold. Drowning ... I had nearly drowned just then. Why did suffocation in quicksand or in some solid substance seem so much more horrible than death by water? I remembered a photograph in an old *Life* magazine. A photographer had been around when a man fell into a silo of wheat. Only his hands were showing in farewell as the photo was taken and he descended out of sight. Like Jaime disappearing into the *cano*.

Surely I could find a better place for a night's rest? I would have to start by making my way round the catwalk. I put off the decision and sat on the sacks in silence wishing that I had bought some cigarettes in the bar. My own were left in the bag under the cork tree.

There was a noise on the far side, as the door through which

I had entered creaked open. When I saw the beam of torchlight I thought that the caretaker must have come up to check after all, and then perhaps that the men who had left the spade and sacks were here to steal more rice. I could hear voices.

"Why in here at all?"

"You saw him go into the yard."

"He could have slipped out again."

Two voices? Three? Two. The torch beam began moving, first high as it played over the ceiling, then in sweeping semi-circles across the bed of rice. It nudged the catwalk with more assurance. Little by little it approached the pile of sacks where I was crouching.

"There!" The light shone full in my eyes.

"*Hombre,* come round here. That is an order." The thick accent sounded local. Unlikely that it belonged to a *guardia civil.* That sort were always imported from elsewhere. I had no idea who these two could be. Local vigilantes? Factory workers? I kept silent and the same voice tried again.

"Come round quietly."

I made no move. Let them sort it out for themselves. They were talking low to each other. They talked for some time. I could hear what they were saying, even though the words were uttered in guttural whispers; voices carried over the rice as if it were water. "*Don Sanchez . . . le echaremos en el roz . . . se escondera el cuerpo . . .*" By the time I realized their purpose it was too late to surrender the way they had first demanded. They should have come armed. Incompetent people as well as cruel. I heard movements down to my left, steps along the catwalk. They might have knives. It is not altogether easy to kill a man without any weapon at all. Except by throwing him off a height. Into space. Into rice. Soon they would come round the corner and then a second one, and come towards me. I felt for the spade lying on the floor, grabbed it and turned to the door behind the pile of sacks, hammering blows where I felt the lock must be. Blows that were loud and urgent, their sounds obliterating the sounds of footsteps on wood. The torch jogged round me. The man who reached me first was the one carrying it. The catwalk was too narrow for both of them to deal with me at once, and I had some advantage, like Horatius on the bridge. There was just enough width for me to meet him with a chopping half swing of the spade, whose flat blade caught him in the side of the head. He staggered back waving his arms, nearly tripping over the man behind. The torch went sailing out of his hands, and sank into the rice, leaving the place in darkness.

The first man was down on the floor now, groaning. But the second did not hesitate. Before the light disappeared he had seen enough of me to plunge forward towards his prey. Then he was at me, trying to down me with a display of all-in wrestling—flailing arms and flat handslapping and fingers gouging. A kick.

The spade was a surprise to him. He hadn't seen it or realized how I had clouted his companion. With an effort I got the cutting end into his chest, pushing him away from me. He was stronger and bigger than I was, but the spade was a grand weapon. I hit him with a blow like a tennis serve. It subdued him for an instant, before he lunged forward again. An arm round my waist, another at my neck. I felt my feet lifting off the floor, and jabbed him ineffectually on the back with the handle. Then I had to throw it down and struggle without it. He was strong. But the blow that I had given him made him a little groggy, not all that groggy so he didn't realize when I won. As I heaved him over the railing with tremendous effort, he screamed, a sound cut off abruptly when he hit the frosty surface of the rice.

There was a pause. The two of us that were left were not quite in darkness or in silence. The torch had not sunk under the way the man had—only a slight layer of rice lay on top of it, like clouds over the moon, and it gave out a faint glow from where it lay buried. There were a number of pattering noises like those made by mice. The rice was resettling. Or *he* may have been moving about underneath, feeling for the bottom, flailing his arms about in a new fluid medium, striking out for the surface.

"Salvador ... Salvador ..." The second man on the catwalk called out in a hoarse voice. He tried again, whispering, "where are you?" I kept quiet. There were more horrible sounds from the bed of rice. Another long pause while he worked out what had happened. I stood motionless against the battered door. Then I picked up the spade, clanking it on the metal at my feet. I could hear him get up and retreat back round the three sides of the catwalk. He went very slowly, limping, and I could hear each step. Careful steps. He was trying not to make a noise. He reached the far door and went out slamming it.

72

I stood for a long time, waiting for the rustles to stop, but they continued, although the spaces of silence between them got longer. This was no place to stay. While the men had been coming round the catwalk, I had nearly broken down the door behind me. Now I lifted the spade and resumed my hammering, not caring if the caretaker should come, or the man who called for Salvador should return with friends and guns. Two hard blows dealt with the lock, and it gave way against my weight. Black darkness. Not a clue as to what there might be—snakes or scorpions. I stepped cautiously to the right, feeling with my hand. Tins . . . a box of nails. Two, three, four open boxes of nails and screws. Some more, cardboard, closed. My hand came to a corner and I had to change direction. More shelves with bottles. A softness at my feet. I bent down and felt more sacks. I knocked over a bottle and it fell with a crack like a shot on to a concrete floor. The faint prosaic smell of turpentine reached my nostrils. Then I felt a door, and rapped it with my knuckles. Metal. Locked on the other side.

I was in a very small storeroom, whose way out was barred; I doubted if I would have been able to break that door down, even if I had the energy to resume beating with the spade. And I had no idea where the darkness might lead. Better the devils I knew. I came out on to the catwalk again, and heaved the spade into the rice, after wiping the handle free of fingerprints with one of the sacks. The buried torch still glowed beside Salvador's grave as I felt my way around and out of the store, groping my way down the stairs. There was one light left on in the caretaker's office. I would push past him and run. But when I came upon him he couldn't sound any alarm. He sat bound and gagged with a brilliant white linen handkerchief. In the struggle to seat and tie him, his hair had become ruffled and was now being blown about by the draught that came through the holes in the window above his table. The glass had been shattered by the arm rests of his crutches as they had been heaved outside. If he should work his way free, it would take him more time to hobble out and find them. They hadn't bothered to tie up his leg, only his arms to the back of his chair. The transistor had been left on for him, and it was playing a song about *Un Millon de Amigos*.

I was shocked to see him. Things had become very complicated for me. He had his story to tell, and sooner or later Salvador would surface.

Two men had tied up the old man. He hadn't seen a third. He had been on his rounds when I slipped through his office. The survivor must have dashed past him and out of the door after Salvador's disappearance. Was it possible that he and the authorities might believe that the night's events were merely a simple break-in by two men? They would not see a third for some time, not until the rice over Salvador was shifted. They might wonder why there had been such a time lag between the departure of the two thieves, but was there any real reason why they should be associated with a rogue foreigner? Unless, of course, the caretaker identified me. His eyes bulged with appeal, but I moved behind him very quickly, hoping that he could not have seen me properly. There was only one way that I could make sure that he could not be a witness against me. Enough of that. The people who had tied him up had ruffled his jacket so that the inside pocket showed, revealing his wallet. I reached over his shoulder and pulled it out. Its removal would make more of an impression of burglars. Besides I should have some more money; my gamekeeper's bribe would just pay the bus fare to Seville. I found a few notes mixed up with some photographs of babies. Grandchildren. He gave out a croak as I threw the wallet on the table in front of him. I bent down and examined his watch, having to turn his bound arm round a little to look at its face. Twenty past three. Four hours until the bus departed for Seville.

In spite of the smashed windows the room felt warm from the stove. There was a chair behind him, and I was tempted just to sit there with the trussed figure beside me and let the hours pass. But that would not help the burglar theory. I left and went out of the factory yard, to spend the rest of the night hanging round the outskirts of Villafranco waiting for dawn. Waves of nausea, actually vomiting. A murder a day. A nasty murder a day. Everything hopeless. Teeth chattering. Towards dawn I began to feel some remorse as well as self pity, and I began to worry about the old man. Would he last out, tied up hour after hour? I hoped so. I thought of the other old man I had killed. In the end I went back.

Actually he was fine. They hadn't tied him too tightly. The

74

transistor was playing Manuel de Falla's Fire Dance. I stood in the same place behind him and then thought about fingerprints on the wallet. I found a duster in his desk drawer and wiped it down. Without letting him see my face. It would make his story more curious, but I was glad I had come back to check.

I went towards Villafranco as the line of rice fields turned gold at the edges from the rising sun. In the town the bars were full again as workmen drank their breakfast. Little to celebrate at that time of day; silent grey faces swallowing Anis and Fundador, small flames that would fuel them through their morning's work. I avoided bars and went into a little shop, where I picked up some chocolate from the display counter, together with a couple of oranges. The girl in the tartan skirt and thick woollen knee socks who served me, yawning, was not at her most alert.

The momentum of the working morning increased. Land-Rovers, Fiats and great trailer lorries with blue tarpaulin covers and names like Roberto, Inceite or Priete zoomed down the street and out into the flat countryside. Becoming bold I bought a news-paper. Then down near the Bar Isla I saw a woman cooking *churros* on an open stove, squeezing out dough into a tin basin filled with bubbling oil. I bought plenty—hot fried rolls. I ate them pacing up and down with almost the same relentless gait as the pair of *guardia* I glimpsed emerging from a side street. Was the bus late? Would it be watched? Men would be at work at the factory within a few minutes. They would find the old fellow tied up.

I could not see any sign of police activity as the red Seville bus swung into the main street and parked with a hiss outside a bar. I joined the queue which was quickly filling it up to go to Coria del Rio or Seville. Housewives carrying bags, farmers in grey suits and Cordoban hats, droves of children. Sevilla? Fifty pesetas. As well that I had the caretaker's money. Would I sit front or back? Either equally unsafe in the event of a search; a bus is a moving trap. I temporized and sat three seats down beside a window. When a woman moved in beside me I pulled out the newspaper and hid behind it.

Several photographs. One was a snap of Patterson with his buzzard taken by Miguel during one of the idle days of autumn. Another showed the magistrate in charge of the case looking aggressively civilian in his white raincoat, as he stood near the cork tree with a group of policemen. There was my photograph again, together with a good deal of newsprint. I had not got a good press. The reporter had roughed out the portrait of a werewolf. He had exuberantly interviewed a lot of people at the palace. Every coldness with Patterson had been resurrected; words and phrases long vanished on the air were remembered with clarity. It seemed that Patterson had spent much of the winter hinting at my ornithological betrayals. No one had believed him, partly because he was disliked, partly because he had no proof.

Here the newspaper showed puzzlement. The Iberian peninsula smouldered with violence, and the reporter had to explain to its readers the nature of my perfidy. In Spain when men didn't kill each other, they killed animals. They continued the passion of their ancestors for slaughtering stag, ibex, roebuck, boar, wolf, bear, mountain sheep . . . not to mention all the fowls of the air. I thought about the writer, Miguel Delibes, who made his reputation by extolling hunting with an enthusiasm exceeding Abel Chapman's gory chronicles. *Alegrias de la Caza, Diario de un cazador, La Caza de una perdiz roja, El libro de la Caza* praised the concept of destroying wild life with the license accorded to English fox-hunting gentlemen. It was hard for Spanish newspaper men to convey to their readers that at the palace a greater revulsion was felt for my theft of birds' eggs than for my assumed murder of Patterson. They were helped somewhat by an hysterical interview with Hubert. After I had departed from the Hafner Hide—(long explanation about its function)—when Dr Patterson had voiced his suspicions that I intended to rob the nest of the imperial eagle—(one of the noblest manifestations of Spain's wild life, alas increasingly rare)—Hubert, to his eternal regret, had not believed him. He had refused to accompany Dr Patterson when the eminent doctor had set out to catch the villainous destroyer of nature at his despicable work . . .

There was much more. A blurred picture of Jaime, and the assumption that his disappearance was connected with mine. The first correct assumption anyone had made. The search of my effects—they had discovered the pale creamy buff sparsely marked clutch of azure-winged magpie eggs that I had lifted from a nest pointed out to me by Miguel. And the rare clutch of seven greenish-blue eggs of *ardea purpurea*, the purple heron. I had speculated that two females had laid them. They had been stored in cotton wool in a wide-mouthed thermos. Even Patterson had not quite had the nerve to search my bedroom. What would happen to them? Someone would smash them eventually. Part of the beauty of eggs was their fragility. Philosophic oologists sometimes speculated that the renewed vogue in collecting black eggs was related to the perishable and uncertain nature of our daily lives. During the war when things were at their most chaotic and unpredictable, there had been a boom in collecting old china. The egg of *aquila heliaca* which I carried round with me seemed increasingly precious the more messed up my existence became.

The bus sped past groves of eucalyptus which set their seal on ground raised slightly above the reclaimed *marismas*. Bulls grazed peacefully behind arched gateways, oblivious of a violent future. A little more straight road and we were on the outskirts of another town. This one, called Alfonso XII, had similar architecture to Villafranco, concrete apartment blocks, grey flat-roofed buildings looking out into dusty streets.

The driver braked suddenly and pulled up behind a large lorry. A funny sort of place for a traffic jam. After the bus had remained stationary for about five minutes the mood of the passengers became lively. Strident voices asked questions. Women tried to squeeze out of their seats, men jumped up to look. The driver released the door so that the conductor could go out and investigate the nature of the hold-up.

I had chosen my seat badly. I would have been better right up front. The old lady beside me was the fattest woman on the bus, and tucked in all round her were specimens of what Americans call Polish luggage—paper bags, plastic bags, carrier bags, boxes. On her lap she clutched a closed basket in which she was transporting a cat. I tried treading on her grey-stockinged instep that bulged out of black shoes, and she cried out with pain.

"But señor, why?"

"Quick . . ."

"Why? . . ."

"I want to buy cigarettes." She moved a little bit, but she was wedged very tight. I found it easier to climb over the high-backed seat in front of me, stepping on the ashtray on the arm rest, leaping over the lap of a priest into the narrow passageway. Of course people began shouting, a different note from the questions they had been directing with such animation at the driver.

These shouts had that urgency that makes one understand why the Spanish put exclamation marks at the beginning of verbal ejaculations as well as at the end. A long-haired youth smelling of lavender water tried to stop me.

"Close the door!" The driver, who had been looking front-wards out of the blue-tinted window at the moment when I started moving, had not yet fully grasped the reason for the commotion. "The door!" the same know-all voice shouted. He understood. But the hiss and snap of pneumatic doors takes a long second—and I was out into the street as the rubber jaws met behind me. Another two seconds passed before the doors concertinad back and a blast of shouting caught the attention of passers-by and the *guardia civil* who were checking the queue of vehicles, peering into each one. Four of them, two pairs. They moved swiftly, their hats glinting in the morning sun. Passengers were pointing towards the crowded pavement, where it was still rush hour; men were on their way to work, and a number of them were wearing boiler suits. Most of the crowd had paused in its movements to stare at the bus, but a number of con-scientious workers were continuing their progress towards their factories. I walked with them as fast as I dared. Behind, at a distance, the shouts were mixed with police whistles and stamp-ing feet. I turned down a side street flanked by small white-washed houses—there were people here too, mostly children carrying school satchels, boys with cropped heads, girls with gold rings and studs in their ears. Some of the boys had sensed excite-ment and were running towards it. I turned down another street, quieter still, with only a couple of women carrying black plastic baskets full of washing, waddling past newly planted eucalyptus trees. Another turn, another street, an alley rather. Two more boys fighting beneath a tattered poster about bullfighting that had endured the winter.

I continued threading through the suburbs of Alfonso XII until I must have circled half the town. I was walking alone now, down another depressed laneway named Calle Fleming after the penicillin patron of matadors and whores. It was about a quarter of a mile long and led away; the houses stopped abruptly as it became another muddy road across another expanse of rice and flood. I walked right to the last house and hesitated before turning and plunging back into the town, now presumably seething with police looking for me. Behind me a big yellow tractor turned into the Calle Fleming and came chugging up. It slowed down and I had nowhere to run.

"You want to walk over there?" The driver bawled down.

I didn't answer, but stood looking at him, mouth open.

"Want a lift to San Martino?" He pointed to a distant smudge of trees on the horizon.

I was deeply suspicious—could he be another of the unknown men who followed me yesterday? To be offered a lift by a stranger was a rare experience in a country where hitch-hikers are non-existent and no self-respecting pedestrian will demean himself by thumbing a passing car. Fools and poor people walked, and criminals sought free transport. The driver was very young, not twenty yet. And this was a brand new tractor. I assumed—because it was the easiest thing to assume during those few seconds—that his pride in riding it, perhaps for the first time on his own, made him wish to share the experience.

"*Muchas gracias,*" I muttered, climbing up behind him.

Chapter five

H E S E E M E D G E N U I N E L Y proud and pleased to have
me as a passenger up on his chariot. I remembered a poem about
a Welshman on a tractor ... something about his nerves of steel
and his blood oil ... something else about riding to work now as
a great man should. He sang a loud nasal song with a refrain in
English—"Relax now Baby!" The noise inhibited conversation.
The tractor went at the pace of a fast stage-coach, more or less
the speed our ancestors travelled when they wished to hurry. We
chugged over the familiar flat fertile landscape with wide views
and blue lights in flooded water reflected from the clear sky. Any
heat from the sun was tempered by the breeze of our movement.
There couldn't be a nicer way to travel. But it was too slow. It
was another manifestation of waking nightmare, as once again,
the speed of the fugitive was unnaturally reduced. I kept turning
my head to look for police cars coming out of the town. Nothing,
merely the long straight track to the Calle Fleming. Slowly the
town behind us shrank, becoming featureless and grey, while the
blur ahead thickened into a line of cottages with straw roofs.
Chozas. Dogs greeted us; two children pulled a small pig led with
rope tied round a hind leg, and a couple of men lying asleep
under eucalyptus trees were woken by the noise we made.

I jumped down hastily. "Thanks friend," adding a reluctant
shout because he seemed to expect it, "You have a fine tractor."

"My pleasure," he bellowed back. I longed to talk to him—
ask him, for instance, where I was. He threw the great orange
machine into a different gear.

"Hey, Julio!" The men under the eucalyptus trees were old;
so were the others who gathered round him with women, children
and dogs. Younger men were away working in Alfonso XII or
Villafranco, or possibly Germany or Switzerland. They pointed
to where the tractor was to go. It seemed that the community
had enough money to contract the driver to plough up the
vegetable patches beside the *chozas*. For this year at least no one
had to embark on rugged spadework.

80

The trip hadn't done me any good. I would have been far better off as a fugitive in Alfonso XII than out in this place. I would have to go back the way the tractor had brought me. What else could I do? Go to the sea? I wondered about the possibilities of reaching Gibraltar. Things had changed since the days when men moved to and from Algeciras with their arms covered with cheap watches. Perhaps I could lose myself on a beach or squeeze in with a coachload? I knew such ideas were aimless. The best plan was the Seville one—even though meeting up with Joaquín would probably be another futile exercise. He might well be in jail himself—liberal lawyers were having a bad time of it at present.

I must move out of this place. If I lingered I would attract attention. The tractor driver had assumed that I was part of the community—soon it would become evident that I was not. I slipped behind the row of cottages where the sandy land was marked out in long rectangular plots, just like suburban gardens. Fences divided them, some of wire, some of prickly pear. They seemed mostly enclosures for washing, which snapped in the breeze. In the first plot nearest me a young woman was getting her linen on to a line, struggling to keep sheets out of the mud. I watched her for some time, freezing behind a eucalyptus tree as if it were the Hafner Hide. She was a stout girl with holes and tears in her black and grey clothes. But her glossy black hair, set in rollers which were almost invisible at this distance, looked ringleted and formal like a court lady painted by Goya. Puppies and a baby were playing near her. She hung out nappies. Behind her, leaning against a clump of prickly pear, was a small ladies' bicycle, old fashioned, so that the descending bar that made room for skirts was rounded instead of angled.

She picked up the baby and lugged it back inside her *choza* in a flurry of puppies. I hoped her housekeeping was absorbing, because there was no way of getting to the bicycle except by climbing over the wire fence that marked out her plot, and moving over her strip of yard. Dogs. True, all the ones I had seen were puppies, but puppies have mothers. I waited five minutes to see if she would come out again, and then went boldly over and climbed the fence. I ran and seized the bike, which, in keeping with its old-fashioned design, was heavy. I lugged it back at a half run and heaved it over the mesh. No dogs barked, but

81

clinging to the fence were two small boys. Very small boys, I was glad to note. One of them was crying because he did not like my appearance. I took out some chocolate and broke off a piece —not too much, since I would need my provisions. I threw it to them, still paper-wrapped and gave them a fierce smile. Then I mounted and pushed off out of that place as fast as I could. Back yards, prickly pear fences and the line of *chozas* concealed me from the tractor and its spectators. But I had a long stretch of cycling during which I would be visible to anyone at the back of the *chozas*.

The bicycle went smoothly; well maintained, it was a tribute to Raleigh whose scratched stencil could still be made out on the frame. It was too small, naturally, and I had to crouch as I pedalled along, composing testimonials for factory workers in Nottingham. Other roads ran into this one in the chessboard pattern I had encountered outside Villafranco. I selected them at random, turning in a series of moves like a knight's in chess. There were no signposts. I wished I had paid more attention during that brief bus ride. Now I was not even sure whether or not I was still on the Isla Major.

Every few minutes I turned and looked back as I had done on the tractor, a movement which slowed me down, but paid off when I glimpsed a shape in the distance growing in the wobbling sun mirage. Although the roads were not tarred, they took a certain amount of motor traffic; since they were raised like causeways over the rice fields, I could carry the bicycle down the bank and hide when any vehicle approached. A car loomed up on an average of every five minutes, and I played safe every time, although I had to risk observation if I passed a building or one of the new farms. There was nothing I could do about the scrutiny of the odd worker or housewife—one woman called out a greeting which I answered with a wave. No pedestrians walked the monotonous length of these roads, but twice Hondas came up and passed me. I hid from both of them.

The sun was overhead when I came to a derelict thatched building that was surrounded by a new experimental farm, whose land had been taken very recently out of the *marismas*. Newly dug canals, pipes and pieces of equipment lying about, and a stream pouring from an open culvert. But something had failed or been delayed; weeds had sprouted and fences were broken.

82

I wheeled the bicycle into an outbuilding with most of the slate tiles missing from the roof, which had been a storeroom and was filled with old packing cases, shredded paper and wadding. I sat down on them, finding them a lot more comfortable than the sacks of the night before, and ate my chocolate. It seemed a lifetime since I had eaten and slept properly. The oranges, which I had bought with the hope that they would quench my thirst, did nothing of the sort; their stickiness merely added to my personal filth. I hesitated for a few minutes, and then went outside to drink long and steadily from the water that came out of the open culvert. Twenty-four hours before I had felt scruples about drinking drainage water.

I did not stay there long. Fatigue and bewilderment were preferable to the depression that rest would bring. Rational decisions were to be postponed yet again. Meanwhile my physical condition was not bad, apart from the odd leech bite and the scratch on my hand. Roaming about Doñana had put me in good shape, The unorthodox schedule of the past two days had affected my body less than a visit to the salt marshes in search of practinoles.

I got back on the bicycle and the dreary road stretched ahead. But over on the horizon there appeared new outlines—the plump profiles of a plantation of stone pines. There was something else in the world besides rice fields; the wilderness was approaching again.

When I found myself on the edge of the *marismas* once more, I felt a delighted familiarity. I watched a herd of fallow deer coming up to feed on the grass-covered edge of this particular stretch of marsh. When my movements disturbed them a dozen heads were raised and I caught two dozen eyes. The birds began again; egrets, ducks and moorhens fed in the shallow water, and in the scrub I glimpsed the yellow flight of a golden oriole. I pedalled along picking out calls, hoots and squawks. The plains of rice were left behind me. The dirt road turned into a sandy track, which was not much good for the bicycle, nor very easy to walk over, wheeling the machine, the rubber soles of my shoes squeaking against the loose sand grains. The path meandered by the marshes through open scrub glowing with yellow halimium and scented with rosemary and lavender bushes. When the sand seemed a little firmer I mounted again and bicycled in and out of scrub along the track. Then I came to a solitary house surrounded by eucalyptus and containing two half-wild dogs, some hens and a small determined-looking woman sweeping the sand outside her front door with a broom made of twigs. God, what lives these women led. I watched her, thinking about her chickens. Could I try and steal one, or using brutal strength force her to kill and cook one for me? How long did it take to cook a stringy, freshly killed fowl? When the dogs started barking, she put down her broom and stood with one hand on a hip, the other shading her eyes. I had met her. I recognized where I was. I could make out the water plants in the silted-up stream ahead of me, one of the many that flowed in and out of the *marismas* and gave its name to this house. Casa de Canada Major. Her husband was another guard who worked on the *Estacion*, and he sometimes brought visitors to see her. Those who were tired of watching birds came here for a chat, a glass of brandy and a chance to take photographs of this aspect of *Andalusie Sauvage*. I toyed with the idea of presenting myself as a lost ornithologist. But by now I must be well known as a fugitive. Her husband would have been bringing her news of the search for me. I could hear flamenco music behind her in the house—her transistor kept her in touch with the world. In addition, I was aware that the out-lying guards' houses often possessed a two-day radio link with the palace—a luxury sanctioned by the World Wild Life people to overcome the problems of difficult communication. She could ring up the palace for a chat as easily as if she were a suburban housewife.

I could not do a detour of her place without getting wet; the Canada Major, however silted up, would have to be forded. Better to ride straight past the house and over the little foot-bridge. She had seen me; she could hardly fail to with the dogs, and she expected me to stop and wish her the time of day. I called out a hasty *buenas dias* as I bounced by, the dogs snapping at the wheels, and did not look back.

At least I had a geographical fix. I now knew that only a short distance away through this forest of scrub and stone pines was the dismal, half-empty little pilgrim town of El Rocio. A place that I had seldom visited during the winter, even though it was reasonably near to the palace. But I had been there enough times for a number of people to know me by sight. Not a place to stay in. The bicycle would get me out of it within minutes, and beyond it was a good main road leading towards the sea.

Meanwhile the going along the bumpy track was becoming increasingly difficult. This morning the bicycle had been an instrument of escape, but right here it was nothing but a liability. For the seventh or eighth time I had to get off and wheel it. I wished I could think of a proper plan of action. There seemed really nothing I could achieve by lingering out of custody except get myself killed by Jaime's murderers. In thrillers the pursued always had objectives. They were getting the secret message or radio scanner from A to B or they were being pursued by the world's secret services, or they were out for wholesome revenge. If they were not acting in a good cause they suffered some ironical and suitable punishment. Like a long stretch in a Spanish jail.

Was there any real point in attempting to reach Joaquín? I might telephone him. Not from El Rocio of course, from that little post office gazed at by the curious. I would hurry through, and then cycle down to the coast, to the new seaside resort of Matalascanas, filled with sun-seeking foreigners.

I was in a position of strength for only another half mile before I discovered why bicycles were rarities around the *marismas*. In the rice area they might be good for transport over the flat land, but here the terrain was against them. The puncture came with such suddenness that I was nearly thrown off. I hardly stopped to examine it, but cut my losses immediately, carrying the machine off the track for a little way, and then hiding it among the spring flowers. Sun rose and rock rose half concealed it, and a clump of iris grew beside it.

So I had to continue on foot, limping a little, new muscles aching. The flies that had been interested in me most of the day were replaced by an evening squadron of mosquitoes. The sight of El Rocio with its back to the marshes was depressing. Previously I had always approached it in a car or Land-Rover and had less time to observe its limitations. The place painfully evoked Abel Chapman's description of eighty years ago: "A squalid hamlet clustered around the chapel of Nostra Señora de Rocio—a more wretched ague-stricken spot we have seldom beheld . . ." Things have changed since his day; people don't get ague any more.

El Rocio has an out-of-season air for eleven months out of twelve. This is because it is a pilgrim town and the pilgrimage takes place once a year at Pentecost. For the rest of the time nothing happens, not even at Easter. Only around Pentecost does El Rico liven up and become quite cheerful as pilgrims from all over Andalusia flock in, mostly on horseback, and pay their respects to the virgin who is known as The Dove or Our Lady of the Dew. They have been coming to her shrine for over seven hundred years; Columbus put off the start of one of his voyages so that his sailors could hurry across the river from San Lucar de Barremada and make special prayers for a safe journey to the Indies.

The track that I had been following—it was no more than that—ended in a huge sandy square named after Cardinal Segura. The area it covered was vast enough by any standards, proportionate to the grandiose monument the despotic old man erected to himself outside Seville. It contained a dense grove of eucalyptus trees which could be seeen for miles, silver-green branches floating high over the rooftops. In summer they threw a welcome pool of shadow on to some of the sand, which was bounded by houses belonging to *hermanidades*. *Hermanidades* are the various pilgrim fraternities, originally derived from medieval guilds, that march during religious processions. They have certain similarities to Orange Lodges, like paying their members' funeral expenses and marching to exhaustion on one day in the year dressed in bizarre uniforms. Those represented here at El Rocio would all walk out at Pentecost. That was three months away, and there was no visible enthusiasm for it yet. All the *casetas* belonging to these fraternities were deserted and locked up; it seemed unlikely that a soul would come near them for another six weeks.

I walked down one side of the square and inspected a row of the little wooden houses, empty as bathing huts in winter. Most of them were box-like affairs with two windows and sometimes a small porch made out of tinted Perspex. One or two were larger and more ornate, decorated with urns and topped with bell towers. The most sumptuous, owned by the *hermanidad* of Seville, had a generously decorated front, a chapel of its own and a large courtyard behind. Its façade was half covered with a curtain of bougainvillaea which hung from glazed flowerpots.

The square was not quite empty. I watched an old lady in black preparing to negotiate the space in her carpet slippers. A man on horseback trotted across, whipping up eddies of sand, and turned down past the *caseta* of the Seville brotherhood. I followed him and watched him disappear down the laneway, his mounted silhouette made sharp against the setting sun like a cowboy at the end of film. To the left off the laneway I noticed a little alley named after Princess Sofia. Queen Sofia, she was by now, but the *hermanidades* had not got round to changing the name. Along one side of the cobbled lane were gardens that spread down from the back of a row of houses in a parallel street, closed off by a low whitewashed wall pierced with wrought-iron gates. On the other side were the backs of the *casetas*. Watched by a couple of cats, I walked down inspecting them ... all tantalizingly attractive, with doors front and back and beds, even lavatories within. All desirably vacant. They were locked in a variety of different ways, some with ancient mortice locks requiring large iron keys, others with simple Yale locks and a few with bolts held together by padlocks. I looked at them carefully, but I could not, as I had done elsewhere, seize an axe or a stone without disturbing someone. The town might appear to be half dead, but a number of people lived in it.

I abandoned that problem and thought about food. Because the scientists living at the palace had to secure their own food supplies, they had got to know the so-called shopping centres of Doñana very well. Most expeditions went to Alamonte, just a few miles from El Rocio—a neat little town with a number of shops used to supplying the ornithologists. I had made a weekly trip to Alamonte since the previous autumn. A bit of meat puzzlingly hacked about by the butcher, some fruit, a tunny-fish or a swordfish steak might constitute an afternoon's shopping, preceding a session of coffee and drinks at a café. Alamonte had several cafés. But no one would think of coming to El Rocio for supplies. Just occasionally, when Hubert and I were in a masochistic mood, we would drive over here for a drink at the bar. As far as I could remember it was the only establishment that sold food here as well. We drank an aperitif here a number of times, and were on smiling *buenos dias* terms with the proprietor. Would he recognize me now, if I went inside and asked for an omelette? Certainly he would.

Nevertheless I moved in the direction of the bar, down a lane which connected the Plaza Segura with a smaller sand-covered plaza, also lined with *casetas* on three sides. Behind them was the tower of the church where the famous little image was lodged. In the centre of the square someone had put up a concrete representation of her, surrounded by six dusty palms, two lights and a *reja* painted silver. The bar-restaurant, named Paloma, after the statute, was on the other side. I sidled up and peered in. It seemed to contain old men mostly, sitting with sticks laid down beside them, fly buttons open to ease protruding bellies. One or two studied football pools. The television showed a panel game. I backed away hastily as a couple of children who had stolen in to watch were ejected. Perhaps I might risk a drink? No chance. Beneath the notice over the bar advertising banquets, weddings and baptisms—festivities that would appear to be seldom celebrated in this company—stood the priest drinking Coca Cola. He had not been amused when Hubert and I had teased him one evening about the exact species of dove the Holy Ghost chose to assume ... and also had continued the same silly game identifying La Blanca Paloma, one of the best known epithets of Our Lady of the Dew.

I continued to peer in, aimless and forlorn as the little match girl. I could see two guards from the palace—Andalusian pastiches, with similar riding jackets, patched trousers, short leather boots and wide-rimmed hats pulled down over their faces at the same jaunty angle. They seemed duplicated, like the tourist junk in the display cabinet beside them—little bronze replicas of the Giralda, alarm clocks, Don Quixote and Sancho Panza carved in wood. A good many guards lived in El Rocio, or nearby. There was another of them, drinking in the corner, another duplicate, except that he was an older man. Retired, probably, living in a small pension. He was having an earnest conversation with someone whose back, facing me, was covered with a pin-stripe suit. Who habitually wore pin-stripe? A half turn of the head. Of course, Dr Horez from the palace. And there was Hubert, sitting right beside him. Too late—he had glanced up and caught sight of me; as I backed away I could see the lugubrious set of his features freeze in an expression of startled recognition.

I walked quickly to the centre of the square beside the statue in its silver fence. Would he help? Would he come out? I'd give him a few minutes. I stood there reading the notice on the railings.

"*En este situo el 8 de Junio 1919 a las once de semana, el emoyrno sur cardinal Doctor Enrique Almaraz y Santos, digimimo Arzabispo de Sevilla corono canonicante a la Santisima Virgin del Rocio antes numerosa concurrencia de devotos...*" I read it five, six, seven times, unaware that I was learning it by heart. Then Hubert came out of the bar and strode over to me. We walked round until the statue and the railings were between ourselves and the bar door.

"Does Horez know I'm here?"

Hubert shook his head. "He's deep in conversation with that old fellow."

"Retired guard?"

"Yes."

"Did you come specially to El Rocio to see him?"

"We were getting supplies in Alamonte, and Horez said he wanted a word with Miguel. Afterwards we're going to have a meal ..." He was nervous, making conversation.

"Rather you than me," I said idly, remembering the tedium of Horez's conversation. We stood silent. At the best of times Hubert's naturally sombre expression combined with the nervous gaiety of a butterfly living through a wet summer. Now the gaiety had departed, and his features underwent a series of exaggerated changes like those of a mime actor. They conveyed amazement, tinged with fear, and then disgust, aggravated by a whiff of mud and sweat. As he took in my appearance, the distaste faded to something I couldn't identify for a moment. Then I did; it was pity.

My own feelings were much simpler. I felt embarrassed. I began to wonder if it would be better if I just walked away rather than endure these curious social agonies. Then my stomach rumbled.

"I didn't kill Patterson."

There was another silence. "Why don't you give yourself up, Lacey?"

"The thing is ... that I didn't kill Patterson."

"For all our sakes ... would it not be better if you went to the authorities with your story?"

"I know I've become an international embarrassment. Giving the *Estación* a bad name ... but I don't want to spend years in a Spanish prison for something I didn't do."

"Naturally, *mon vieux*. But you must sort things out in a rational atmosphere. You are doing yourself no good ... and of course we will all stand by you ..." Testimonials from colleagues —in the avian world I was still a man of distinction. In my Dr Jekyll role I had written a classical textbook. "But nothing can be investigated properly while you persist in this futile evasion of responsibility."

"Do you believe me? That I didn't kill Patterson?"

"Perhaps ..." He had the soothing tone of a wicked old nurse.

"It was Sanchez and a couple of bravos he had with him."

"Sanchez?"

"Yes, you know ... Don Sanchez ... the Maharajah with the white jodhpurs and the expensive sporting guns ... Horez's pal ... the man you love to hate." Hubert's features changed abruptly to an expression which meant "Balls!"

"I swear to God, Hubert, it was the Maharajah. I was a witness to Jaime's murder ... or rather disposal ..."

"Jaime?"

"Jaime Mendoza ... the guard ..."

"The one they are looking for now."

"I suppose they think I killed him as well as Patterson."

He didn't answer.

"I know where he is ... I saw it all ... from the tree while I was egg collecting ... I had the binoculars ..."

Amazingly I read his new expression as "It's just possible". Every ornithologist must see a good deal of extra action quite unconnected with bird life. The number of human courting couples, for example, whom he is forced to observe might make a statistic that would fit in with spring migratory behaviour. "But Lacey, whatever the truth is, you must go to the police without delay."

Another long silence. I said, "Perhaps in the words of John Stonehouse I am committing psychiatric suicide." A remark I regretted instantly. "Look, I just want more time to think."

He shrugged.

"Will you help me?" I tried a Gaelic appeal. "For the sake of our old friendship."

"What do you want?"

"Food. A torch. Food mostly . . . I haven't eaten properly for days . . . and cigarettes and matches."

"If I get you some food now, will you surrender?"

"Later I will. I am much more rational than you think. But don't go calling up anyone now or telling Horez. Trust me, Hubert, please."

"I shouldn't . . . you wait here." He turned and went off across the square. Was he going to where his old Deux Chevaux was parked, or would he go on and get some official help? Evening was being heralded, not only by the noise of roosting starlings, but by the emergence of the *paseo*, if the three youths with transistors and the four fat girls in black could be so described. Any of them might recognize me. This was a decision I was leaving entirely to Hubert. And when he came back in a very short time carrying a parcel, I had mixed feelings. He also brought a loaf of bread, a torch, a packet of Rothmans, a book of matches and a bottle of cognac. The parcel was covered with French postage stamps, and I remembered one of his eccentricities. He couldn't live entirely on Spanish food. It was rumoured that Rosita, the cook at the palace, moved by patriotism and humiliation, spent tearful hours trying to emulate French cuisine. Useless; Hubert secured sustenance from back home in Limoges, and food parcels arrived every fortnight. This must be the current one, collected from the post office in Alamonte. I had seen what previous packages contained. Hams and pâtés.

"I'll need a tin opener."

He hesitated before reaching to his waist where a knife was attached to his belt by a cord and dog lead head. It was shapeless and heavy, loaded down with blades.

"I am as mad as you."

"Perhaps you think there's some truth in my story?" He was silent again. "Try, Hubert, try. There are harder things to believe. Wouldn't it be much more pleasant to think of Sanchez as a murderer than your old friend?"

He relaxed a little. "How can I begin to do so when I am in the company of that old snob Horez?"

"Will you do another thing for me?" He gave me a look of exaggerated interrogation. "Look after this . . ." The polystyrene box had been a nuisance for days. He opened it and examined the egg which had survived intact.

"You'd rather I had murdered Patterson than taken that?"

He did not answer. Not only had I stolen eggs, but eggs of birds of prey which were at particular risk. Shooting, trapping, elimination of environment, and pollution by organo chlorine pesticides destroyed predators in heaps all over the world. I added, "Let me put it less crudely. The eagle is a more beautiful bird than the dodo was. There are plenty of people like Patterson still around."

He managed a laugh. "You may be interested to know that the eagle is continuing to sit."

"I thought it might."

"You did, did you? The bird has a greater brooding instinct than a bantam. Remarkable. It survived all the tumult of the investigation. The palace is in chaos—you have no idea. Police of course. And reporters. Several from English newspapers. The usual Italian photographers."

"What are they doing? Taking pictures of Josefina?"

"Among other subjects there must be countless endearing shots of that spoilt animal. They photographed everything within sight. Scene of crime, shots of brooding eagles, until they were chased off. And now, do you know something really disgusting? After all that, the Danes—did you meet them?—they are insisting on going ahead and building the hide so that they can make their film."

"Why don't the *Estación* people do something to prevent it?"

"The usual reasons. Money—a lot of money is involved. And prestige—you know all the prizes Sigurson got for that sensational film about *melierax metabates*—what is the idiotic name you have for it in English?"

"The dark chanting goshawk."

"On the strength of that old film he has a lot of funds promised from television people all round the world. He's also tapped the Danish government."

"Why does it have to be *aquilla heliaca adalberti*? There are plenty of other predators he could film."

"It has to be the imperial eagle. Something everyone recognizes. A poignant symbol of our vanishing wild life."

92

I was hardly the person to make ethical judgements about conservation.

"There was a big argument about this—a big row." Hubert looked sheepish.

"The night Patterson was found, you mean?"

"Some of us were ashamed of this afterwards. The outcome was that these Danes got their way. And they set off building the hide just as they planned—taking some additional care, you understand, working at night. And the miraculous thing is that the birds continue to brood. Sigurson has fantastic luck."

"In spite of not being left alone?"

"I do not think for a single moment. I thought of writing a paper about it. But of course Sigurson will have all the material and observations. I think he likes the agitation—about Patterson. He'll work that into the film, you'll see, because he is basically a vulgarian."

"He'll kill the goose laying the golden egg. She'll shy off at the last moment . . ."

"It will be interesting to see . . ." He suddenly remembered there were more immediate subjects for conversation. "Lacey, you must take your story to the *guardia civil* . . . I beseech you."

"You wouldn't turn me in yourself?" He would, of course. "Listen, I know I'll have to give up. Let me do it in my own time."

He gave something like a sigh, turned abruptly and walked back in the direction of the bar. I stood balancing all the awkward things he had given me, wondering what to do next and feeling conspicuous after I glimpsed another acquaintance stroll by— the young mechanic at the garage. I turned round beside the silver fence and read about the most worthy Archbishop of Seville yet again. Then I felt the rain on my cheek.

The light drizzle was enough to clear the *paseo* and send people indoors. By the time I had walked up the street and out into the Plaza Segura, the sandy space was deserted except for a bent old woman going away from me with a stick and a sack. Carrying my burdens, I passed the shuttered *hermanidades*, each with a name over the door . . . La Palma de Condado, Hermanidad de Triana, Sanlucar de Barremeda, Jerez de la Frontera. In places tiled pictures of the Virgin had been set in the walls, together with the names of their donors. "*Todo por la Virgin del Rocio.*

Hermano Major. Miguel Baez." "*Bitril. Huelva.* 1970–71." The rain had hurried on the dusk and the starlings were settling down irritably in the trees. It was almost dark when I reached the end of the square and turned down the alley I had inspected before. Not wishing to use the torch, I went down the cobbles, peering at the locks on the back doors of the *hermanidades*. I started when I heard a clatter and saw a swiftly moving shape. A cat or a rat. I moved on and then halted before a door which was locked with a bar and padlock.

I put down the parcel and supplies on the ground, except for the bread which I wrenched into two pieces and thrust in behind the zip of my boiler suit. It had been getting wet. I switched on the torch, and squatting down on the ground so that I could get Hubert's knife into its beam, I tried to find a blade that would serve my purpose. I unravelled a corkscrew, then a marlin spike and a promising object buried deep in the horned handle that proved to be for whipping tops off beer bottles. A hook like a witch's finger would open tins later on. Cursing the insane Formosan cutler, I wrenched open blade after blade. I found nothing like a proper screw driver, but one eventually fitted into the screws that held the bolt in place.

I worked feverishly, using as little light as possible, pausing every few minutes to listen for noises. The worst dangers were from the houses opposite behind the wrought-iron gates and long gardens. The rain grew heavier, insulating sound, and the citizens of El Rocio resigned themselves to the curfew imposed by yet another evening of winter weather. So I hoped.

It took ten minutes to pull out the screws that held the bolt across the door and door post. Six out of eight had to be wound loose and wrenched away from the wood. Inside, the little refuge that I had gone to such trouble to break into was not luxurious. The room that I chose to make my headquarters was on the ground floor; it contained a couple of iron beds with tired mattresses overlooked by an oleograph of La Blanca Paloma. There was a washstand where I could obtain a drink out of the tap. A shuttered window looked out on the square, and behind it a crude *reja* prevented any exit that way. The front door was fastened with a padlock. Only one escape—the way I had come in.

Ignoring the fact that the torchlight must be visible to passers-by, I opened up Hubert's parcel. A lot of it consisted of cheese. A Camembert decorated with a laughing monk, another with a gaily coloured picture of a wren, not drawn well enough for definite ornithological identification. A long log-shaped piece of goat's cheese sprinkled with something that looked like chocolate chippings. The tins contained delicacies like truffled Périgord goose pâté and Strasbourg ham. Everything was rather fatty eaten in large quantities. With the aid of the bread I consumed a tin of pâté, one of ham, and a Camembert and a half. Then after a pause for brandy I finished half the goat's cheese. Although I made myself eat slowly, I felt rather sick.

I lay on the bed, smoking and sipping brandy. I had put out the torch and only the glow of the cigarette lit the darkness. Sleep stole over me. I took another swig and began to wonder if the *hermanidad* might rise to a pillow. There were no blankets, but I had not felt the need for them yet. A pillow would be pleasant.

The darkness was broken by a strong regular flashing light in the square outside, pieces of which filtered through the shutters beside me. I rolled off the bed and peered out at a crack in the side. The searchlight was balanced on top of a military-looking vehicle and swept round the square, piercing the rain, occasionally picking out uniformed figures I heard a siren wail.

Damn Hubert. He had just given me time to finish my supper. Had he first eaten his own evening meal? Hours had passed since our discussion in the square. Had he sat with Horez somewhere in Jerez, worrying about giving me supplies, and what was more, a lethal weapon. But why wait so long? Time for a long talk with Horez. To begin with he'd have to explain the disappearance of his supplies. Our old friendship ... my weakness. Poor Lacey. Pathetic. Loco. Dangerous? Do you think he's dangerous, Doctor? Of course badly in need of medical and psychiatric attention. Does he strike you as a psychotic personality? Of course I acted hastily in helping him. Yes, you are right, most unwise ... for his own good ... waiter, hurry up with that coffee ...

Had it happened like that? Or had Hubert returned to the palace and phoned from there? Not that it mattered. I burst out of the broken door into the alley. Out of the *hermanidad*, where I would have been trapped instantly. Already at the end of the alley a torch was playing on each door to see if any of the locks had been broken. I ran the other way, my gymshoes silent on the wet sand. I was hugging the brandy bottle.

The rain kept the crowds down. No one already in nightwear was going to come out of their front doors to stand in the downpour or help in the chase. Occasionally an upstairs window opened and a sharp or a sleepy voice would call down and ask what was going on.

Sometimes there would be no answer, only the sound of rain in the gutters counterpointing the rush of boots and the siren's wail. Someone who could not resist the call of excitement would answer ... "The *Estación* business ... the murderer ..." But there were too few people living in the pilgrim town to generate much interest, even with the police and sirens. In the rain and darkness I managed to sidestep the small crowds and find myself alone. Opposite me was a line of Urinarios situated by the church. Four Señoras and four Caballeros. About a hundred yards away was the main road out of El Rocio, but between me and that escape was the guard's barracks.

I had three choices, two of which were lingering in the jacks and going down and giving myself up. That old resolution had been shaken again by my conversation with Hubert, and also by the confidence induced by the brandy. I held the bottle tight; I would not surrender my freedom lightly. The rain plastered down my hair and seeped into the collar of the boiler suit. The main door of the church was opposite; I waded across and lingered beside the notice pinned on the baize. *Por Modestia y Dignidad y por respeto a la Virgin y al santuario entren correctamente vestidos.* The door was open. Did it never close? A place where you could go in for a prayer at one or two in the morning, unlike most modern Christian churches that kept shop hours? There were dim lights inside. I had thought it empty, but then I was glad that I endeavoured to make no sound as I slipped in. An old man stood up front polishing something with a rag; the *reja* in front of him cutting off the altar was a high lance-headed railing. It guarded Our Lady of the Dew, the White Dove, the Queen of the *Marismas*.

The man was dressed in a robe, but I didn't think he was a priest. A sacristan, a holy caretaker, privileged to look after the little medieval image which had once been hidden in the hollow of a tree so that the Moors couldn't destroy her. A shepherd had found her. In many parts of Spain statues were discovered in similar circumstances that were considered miraculous—charming miracles that reflected the joy of rediscovered religions after the Moors had been thrown out.

While he had his back to me I made my way around to a side aisle where a line of confessionals stood. I tried the penitent's side of the first of them and didn't like it at all. A miniature of the *hermanidad*, a smaller securer trap. But it hid me when the sacristan turned round. Then he wandered off into the wings, so to speak, with his brush and pan and polish.

There were a lot of things behind the *reja* that I could see dimly which appeared to be big, bulky and concealing. I ran over and clambered over the five-foot-high railing. A massive altar behind, topped with the Virgin clasping her Child and sitting in a silver processional chair. Dim electric light picked out high-lights and jewels from her mantle. The mantle covered the top part of a vast gown of starched tulle. There was plenty of space behind the chair, and the tulle fell in a great concealing curtain.

The heavily embossed silver chair isn't supposed to have much secular handling. The men of Alamonte, the senior branch of the *hermanidades*, are allowed to carry it around during the Pente-costal procession. Perhaps I had been in their little house? It would be pleasant to have some association with them. Otherwise—

> Nadie toque a la Virgen
> nadie se atreva
> que son hombres de Alamonte
> los que llevan . . .

Peering out from behind the statue I could see the sacristan come out and wander down the long aisle to the west end. Before he got there I heard the faint baize-muffled thud as one of the entrance doors opened and shut. Two figures. The guard with the machine-gun crossed himself before he spoke.

"I am just closing."

"Has anyone been in here?"

"No."

The guard paused. Then he went round to the confessionals and peered into each one. His friend stayed near the main door while he looked into the sacristy, switching on a bright light. Then he wandered back until he was beneath the screen in front of the altar. He paused and I hoped that he was merely looking up at the little round-eyed doll in the gorgeous clothes. There was a moment of stillness. The Virgin del Rocio had performed many miracles in her time. Now she arranged another one. He crossed himself again and went down the aisle.

"Lock up carefully when you finish."

"I do so every night."

Lights went out, locks clicked. Perhaps a sanctuary lamp gave out a glow? I didn't notice, for crouching behind the chair I was drinking brandy. I heard the rain outside and felt oddly cosy— perhaps this was the idea of medieval sanctuary. I had no thought of sacrilege, even though the deep sleep I fell into was partly drunken. When I woke in daylight I had a rusty mouth and a headache.

After about five minutes I sorted out where I was, and then realized that just like last night I couldn't get out from behind the Virgin's skirts without being seen. There was a noise like a lion purring coming from just across the way. I took a quick look out and saw the priest kneeling at the altar. He was saying his office. The sacristan was out there beyond the *reja*, sweeping. Another new day for La Paloma. Like most Spanish churches the place had a perpetual gloom, but there was an indication of bright sunlight outside. When one of the doors at the west end opened the quality of light changed just a little.

Two old women with black lace handkerchiefs on their heads entered and crossed themselves and knelt to the Virgin before finding places to sit. Then a *vaquero* came briskly down the side aisle past the confessional and entered the front pew where he knelt and said a long prayer. I could hear continuous thudding of the door as more people came in. The priest was now laying out a white cloth for mass. Soon there was quite a large congregation. Was it Sunday? I had lost count of time. Or was this the usual weekday gathering of housewives, some young girls, and a sprinkling of old men? I peered round for another look. Then I noticed another member of the congregation, a young man standing at the extreme end of the *reja* looking at the altar. Looking below the silver chair, not up at its occupant. At that angle I was visible if I moved or was careless. And I did move.

He turned towards the man kneeling in the front row and nodded his head. I recognized him. Dark, dirty looking. A Roman nose. The charcoal burner.

The priest had started off now and was reading the epistle, while the congregation, hung with rosaries, looked up either at him or at the object of Andalusia's devotions, the Virgin of El Rocio. But the two in front were looking downwards—at the tulle curtain, at the point where the spaces behind the statue vanished from their field of vision.

What had brought them here so certainly when the police had given up? Had they seen me vanish into the church the night before, and been unable or reluctant to come in after me because of police activity outside? Or was it merely that their search was more thorough—that the police had concluded that the report of my presence in El Rocio was a false alarm? For whatever reason the official search for me seemed to have slackened.

How many other friends did the charcoal burner have? I wondered if he and his companion proposed to kill me before the altar like Thomas à Becket or a Florentine despot. Hardly in front of so many witnesses. They were not going to seize me in the name of the law. They would wait until the church was empty. They had all day. After mass some old lady might linger to pray, and others would drift in and out. But sooner or later if these two stayed in the front pew for long enough they would be alone with me. Apart from the image over the altar there would be no witnesses.

A bell tinkled and a few people came up to the altar rail. The two grey men in front sat rigid, staring at the tulle curtain. I thought of trying to mingle with the congregation while it was fluid. Then I thought I would just run. There was a drop of brandy left; I unscrewed the tin top of the bottle and drank it off. I mumbled something to the Virgin—what the harm? No special time seemed good. I counted three and moved, running down the two steps, past kneeling figures and the priest with the cup in his hand and through the gate of the *reja*. I did not run down the aisle, but turned sharply towards the sacristy. It was a risk, but I knew that the charcoal burner had come in that way, and there must be an exit. I ran too hard to hear gasps or horror and cries of sacrilege or to see what movement the watching grey men made.

The sacristy contained a couple of ancient carved chests under a shelf of black books. Also pictures of former priests in gold frames. I looked round. Some photographs had been treated with a process that made them look like oleographs; there was even a saintly light painted in behind them which seemed to give the sitters a rank beyond their station. Others were modern studio portraits. One, informal and slightly blurred, showing a young man in a soutane standing under a tree, hung by itself. It looked nineteen-thirtyish, and I wondered if it depicted someone who had been shot. At last I located the heavy oaken door, hard to see in the dim light, as it was half concealed by some long black garments. The lever handle, set in a brass-mounted lock, opened to a touch. I pulled out the old-fashioned iron key, and pushed it in again outside. It turned easily, just as there were footsteps behind. The sacristan did his job efficiently and the lock was well oiled.

The grey men would have to go round to the front of the church to chase me further. They would have to pass the barracks. Like me, they did not want involvement with the authorities.

Once again I was in the little square with the Paloma's statue. I ran over to the far side towards the stagnant edge of the *marismas*. A dead end, unless I contemplated escaping through water again. There it was along the edge of the square, past some empty reed *chozas* and a line of trees. My nemesis. The tributary of La Madre de las Marismas flowed somewhere beneath it. The reed bed on either side of it would be alive with aquatic nesting birds. Abel Chapman used to endure the ennuis of El Rocio to shoot grebes and herons right here, and eighty-five years later they were still living in the thick brown water choked with mud, frogs and leeches.

Why go to trouble? Give yourself up. When I turned round in the direction of the church and the barracks, I saw the charcoal burner and his friend running towards me. No one with them. My strategy in timing my escape for the high point of the mass had meant that they could chase after me alone. Leave it to us, father, these good people need not be disturbed. The congregation with its rosary beads would be slow to move out and make an inquisitive crowd mixed with policemen, and there was some time for the men to catch up with me. By the time a crowd had gathered I would be dead.

The Opel was parked in the far corner of the square, its owner beside it drinking from a flask. As I ran towards it I made out that the little white oval hovering over the number plates contained a capital D. The migratory movements of German tourists are as far flung as those of Arctic terns.

Would I steal the car? Obtain a lift by force? I stopped, took out Hubert's knife and snatched open a blade. One of the smallest of the knife's selection, but there was no time to try for anything more menacing. I ran towards the man with the flask.

He was young with long blond hair reaching down to his shoulders. He wore skin-tight jeans and a T-shirt decorated with a comic strip. "Zap!" said Captain Midnight, striding over his chest. When he saw me he was surprised and then he was very frightened.

"¡Entra en el coche!" I shouted, waving the knife. He responded immediately; international terrorism has developed instinctive reactions.

"Drive out of here."

He could see the two men running behind, who must be at the statue by now. I wasn't turning round. He took a maddening extra two seconds to empty the coffee out of his flask lid and screw it back on. I had time to decide whether to get in beside him in front or in the back. In front I could keep the knife near him where he could see it. In the back there was a sleeping bag along with a couple of suitcases. He had slept by the roadside and had not done any tidying up. I might get the best of all possible worlds and escape completely.

I was in the back behind him, glaring at him in the mirror, holding up the knife. He was so nervous that the starter scratched away a couple of times without result. We could hear footsteps now, muffled by sand. A hand tugged at the door beside me. I slammed down the lock mechanism. The car moved forward with a jerk.

"Acelerar!" I shouted, emphasis on the lisped syllable coming out in balls of sputum. The tyres shrieked as he revolved the wheel sharply, changing the angle of movement. The man with his hand on the door fell back in the dust as we moved forward in diagonals. I looked back; he lay twisting in agony, the back wheel having gone over his foot. I felt pleased.

"Straighten up." The charcoal burner followed doggedly for a few minutes and then stopped.

"Get me through the town." The driver's nervousness continued to show, and I was afraid that his trembling would make us stall. I settled down between front and back seats with the sleeping bag on top; someone might remember that the German tourist had entered El Rocio without a companion. Had they the place cordoned off? Where were the sirens and searchlights of last night?

I felt the corner of a book sticking into me. I shifted it and saw a title in Gothic German letters indicating that it was the diary of a revolutionary. Leila Khalid? Someone associated with Baader Meinof? Old Che? I didn't have time to browse. But it gave me an idea ... not a particularly good one, since now was scarcely the time to start testing my driver's revolutionary zeal. During the last couple of days, thanks to my Celtic colouring, half-grown beard and stolen boiler suit, I had managed to pass unnoticed as a Spaniard. Could I pretend ... I shifted the sleeping bag and hissed up at him:

"I am a Basque patriot. The police want me." I tried to make my voice as guttural and convincing as possible. Impossible to tell if he steadied after that. He hated the knife. But at least the car continued to move.

Then it slowed down.

"*Polizei*, ..." his voice trembled. The *guardia civil* barracks were ahead. "Go on," I said, "not too fast ... if they challenge you, stop." The last thing I wanted was a speed-up. I got down out of sight, mentally shrugged and left it to him. Give him a moment longer. If he stopped I would come up hands in the air. Better than receiving a couple of red-hot bullets through the car's steely sides. I had achieved what I wanted—had saved my own life. Was the bonus of escape from El Rocio worth any extra gamble?

The Opel moved forward smoothly. It seemed that no one had taken any notice of us.

"We are out of the town now." His Spanish was competent but hesitant, not as good as my own. "Keep on driving," I told him. A very short time had elapsed since I ran out of the church. Five minutes possibly? Not much more. With one bound Carruthers had broken free. For a minute or two I lay wedged in the back, my thoughts diverted by Carruthers. When did he first become a joke? As far as I knew no one in John Buchan's books bore his name. There must have been a time around the beginning of the century when a hero could be called that without embarrassment. The narrator in *The Riddle of the Sands* was Carruthers. Didn't Alec Waugh use the name in his schoolboy novel, *The Loom of Youth* ... Gordon Carruthers. Perhaps the sniggers began there. Dame Carruthers in *The Yeoman of the Guard* could scarcely count. If I ever got out of here, I would look up the London telephone directory and see how many Carruthers's there were in that. Why was the name more foolish than—say—Carstairs?

"We are on the main road now."

"Do not stop." I sat up and looked out. A juggernaut with corrugated steel sides passed with a roar that made us both jump. I made a show of closing up Hubert's knife and throwing it down on the seat beside him. The flask was there, and I picked it up and poured coffee into the lid. "Want some?" Keep the dialogue brief. He shook his head. I drank. "Where does this road lead?"

"To Matalascanas." Of course—to Andalusia's newest coastal resort.

"Are you planning to stay there?"

"For a short time." He sounded reassured. "You said you were a Basque?"

"Yes." It didn't matter now what he took me for. But he didn't question me further. We drove in silence, passing the turn off for the *Estacion* with its sign, *"Carretera Particular. Prohibido el Paso"*. Further on, towering white buildings loomed out from sand dunes. A few years ago the land on which they had been built was as wild as the rest of Doñana. The development of Matalascanas was the most recent result of powerful commercial pressure. Naturalists at the *Estación* had watched painfully and wasted a lot of time sending reports to government departments and lobbying ministers in Madrid. They had tried to publicize the consequences of breeding decline among birds and the dangers to conservation rising out of new towns using up large quantities of water needed in the preservation of the *marismas*. And here was the result of their efforts. Matalascanas was heralded by a series of noticeboards most of which advertised wooden holiday bungalows. "Maribu—Terra Atlantica." "Chalet Hawaii." "Chalet Sunshine." The big developments, the tower block hotels, had greetings in five languages on double-sided noticeboards. One side said *Bien Venido*, Welcome, *Bienvenu*, *Willkommen* and so forth, the other Come again and *Au revoir* and the rest. Like Babel.

We drove through vistas of sandy beach, half-finished roads and footpaths, supermarkets, bars and newly planted palm trees.

"Have you anywhere to go?" he asked.

"No."

He hesitated. "You could stay with me for a day or two."

"No."

"I would like to help you."

"This is no game. The police are savages." He just grinned. I stated some of my real objections. "You are going to a hotel. I have no documents."

"The manager is a friend of mine. I knew Kurt when he ran a hotel in Ibiza. Always accommodating . . . a friend in trouble he will always help." Anything from drugs to a skimpy bikini. But there must be limits. "He never asks for passports the first day . . . My room will have two beds . . ."

We had stopped outside the Hotel Miramar. A bed. I felt weak and longing.

I nodded wearily. As he got out of the car, he took Hubert's knife and pocketed it.

I lay back contemplating the rows of glossy cars that proclaimed all was well with the German motor industry. Occasionally someone youthful and Teutonic strolled through the car park carrying beach things and wearing a tan that proclaimed all was well with the Spanish spring tourist season. My friend took a long time to return. In a few seconds I would probably hear the noise of police sirens. The manager would have talked sense into him, Kurt his name and probably his manner.

I was asleep when my arm was shaken.

"I am taking my suitcase through the front. Later I will come back for you."

"Have you told Kurt?"

"Not everything."

He went away and I slept again. I started awake when he knocked on the window pane beside me with his knuckle. He was a fool. He could be shoved into jail for years without trial. He grinned as I stumbled out on to the concrete parking lot, and beckoned me to follow him.

Chapter six

THE HOTEL WAS trimmed with zig-zags as if giant pinking shears had been at work. Roof tiles and staircases were duplicated to contrast with the egg-box effect of private terraces pushing out from sea-facing rooms all along the cliff that stretched by the beach. It seemed as white and as massive as anything overlooking the English Channel and undulated very slightly around one side of an irregularly shaped verdigris swimming pool.

We made our way through a side door that led into a fitness centre. Then along a tiled corridor past doors marked with simple symbols indicating lavatories, a musical club and a discotheque. Inside the musical club someone was plucking at a guitar. No Spaniard. It always seems effrontery for a foreigner to bring his guitar to Andalusia. Patterson had one, and often used to afflict the palace residents with folk songs featuring the whining regrets of condemned felons, ruined maids or dying engine drivers. Occasionally we passed a fair-haired child or a plump adult with red and peeling skin. There were perhaps a dozen more people in beach clothes in the foyer, drifting under the heavy Teutonic chandeliers. I followed my companion up the main stairs, hoping I would be mistaken for a workman. The place had been built very recently and plenty of things were not quite finished. Knots of wiring protruded from walls and ceilings. The spring sun had not yet dried out the smell of damp cement on the fourth-floor landing, and the window beside the staircase which looked westward on to the hotel next door, which had been designed by an equally aggressive architect, was misted over. Perhaps in shame.

The corridor contained something like fifty doors, each with phoney Moorish panelling. Presumably the rooms had similar decor to the one in which we locked ourselves—curtains patterned with imitation leopard skin, good quality orange carpeting whose colour withstood to some extent the sunlight that came in across the balcony. Above the beds was a print of two flamenco dancers threatening each other with castanets.

He unpacked, throwing clothes into the wardrobe, lending me this electric razor, a jar of Badedas and a knee-length yellow towelling bathrobe. The shave was good. The bath, located down the corridor, contained a number of gold pubic hairs and the water was tepid. It was the biggest disappointment of my life. But the exercise had astringency value, and I got some of the dirt off.

Back in the bedroom I found that he had ordered a meal for me—frankfurters, mashed potato, sauerkraut, a vinegary salad and cold caramel custard. A glass of lager. I wolfed it down while he talked. I learned that his name was Hans and he was a commerce student. Being a student meant that he was chronically short of money. Travel was an increasingly expensive luxury in inflation-torn Europe and confined to countries where the exchange rate was favourable. Spain's recent devaluation meant that a holiday here was still a bargain; even so he would not be able to stay long in this resort in the comfort to which he was accustomed. It did not seem a topic designed to impress a Basque revolutionary, but I was too tired to care and punctuated his grumbling with yawns. In spite of my nap behind La Paloma's chair, I was totally exhausted. Once or twice he looked as if he was about to start asking questions; but I did not have to pretend that I was speechless with fatigue. Finally he gave the conversation up.

"You sleep. I am going out to the pool for a swim and perhaps some frauleins. My own girl friend will not be arriving for two days. She is a receptionist with Lufthansa. She gets all her fares paid for." I was reassured, because I had begun to wonder whether he might be homosexual. No one with a modicum of intelligence could take my story seriously, and what was more, propose to help me. Probably he was going to get in touch with Kurt and then with the authorities. Could there be a reward for my arrest? Anything so long as I slept first.

It was dark when I woke and the main light was on. Hans was standing by the door into the corridor which was ajar. He peered out, down both ways, and shut it carefully.

"The *guardia civil*. They are searching the hotel. They have been searching every hotel in Matalascanas."

That was that. Sleep had been too much of a luxury. A relief in many ways.

"The corridor has guards at each end. You will have to get into the cupboard."

I protested sleepily but he was insistent, whispering how he would be in trouble when I was caught. At last it had occurred to him. He bundled me into his ugly wardrobe, which had the same type of Moorish panelling as the door. Ignoring my expressions of regret, he turned the imitation antique key in the ornate lock. There was a smell of new planed plywood and of dry cleaning liquids off his clothes. Couldn't they be lethal in some circumstances—such as close confinement? Through the leaf-shaped keyhole, mostly filled with the key, I could see a patch of red which I did not identify—then I realized that it was part of the dress of one of the flamenco dancers in the print over the beds. I squatted down uneasily among Hans's chukka boots and sandals.

There was silence for up to ten minutes, and then sudden voices as the door opened from the corridor. Hans chatting in German, a girl laughing. She laughed more loudly after the chink of glasses. A lot of glass chinking, then a little less talk and laughter and the creak of bedsprings. I brooded in my crouching position, like Patterson in a hide observing the courtship of *podicipedidae*.

The knocks and tramping could be heard several doors down. Hans and his girl took no notice until they stopped just outside, and then made no haste to answer the summons. A pause and new sounds above Hans's "Bitte?"

An effusive apologetic manager's voice speaking German. Could this be Kurt? Much chinking of his master keys. Neutral police voices. No embarrassment—why should there be after inspecting a thousand foreign-occupied bedrooms, many of them kept locked by athletic young people making love? Someone's boots moved towards the balcony and darkness blotted out the flamenco dancer's dress. A pause; a door slammed.

Hans and his girl argued. She was happy to stay where she was, but I gathered that Hans was trying to convey that he had been distracted. He mentioned, mumble mumble, "Discotheque". Water splashed in the basin and there was more movement in front of the flamenco frills. She sounded peevish as they moved towards the door; her voice was cut off when it slammed.

Would he leave me inside here all night? Better by far the cold spaces behind a church altar for bedding down. But no, he was a good fellow. He came back into the room having made some excuse. He flicked the key in the lock and went away again. I waited for a little time and then opened it. In the darkness I could make out the shape of the beds. I tottered over to the one I had slept in before, which seemed to be getting all the action. I lay down, but not to sleep. Perhaps the fumes of carbon-tetrachloride from Hans's clothes kept me awake.

The authorities were searching for me now. They had been searching for me last night at El Rocio with sirens and search-lights. Presumably because Hubert had reported my presence there. But between the two searches there seemed to have been a strange gap. The sirens had been called off at El Rocio. And it must have been well known that I was in the area. Hubert had seen me. And I had broken into one of the *casetas* of the *hermanidades*.

I could only think of one reason why the search at El Rocio would be called off. And that was if I had been reported else-where. By someone quite certain of my identification. An authoritative witness with some sort of proof.

But Hubert? He had actually talked to me. How could his story be discredited? A reliable scholar, with Dr Horez to back him up. Respected Dr Horez, a local and eminent figure. Another scholar, like we all were. A friend of Don Sanchez's . . . running to bow and shake hands every time he appeared at the palace.

I broke into a sweat and sat up and switched on the bedside light. My mind swiftly plotted out a nasty scenario. Hubert, after seeing me and giving me the food I asked for, going off and confiding in Horez. Telling him what I had told him—what I had seen from the cork tree. I had identified Sanchez. Suppose Sanchez's friend, Dr Horez, was more than a friend? An ally as ruthless as he was? Men had already died so that I should not report my story. Perhaps Hubert had become another corpse?

Suppose Hubert had talked to Horez. Horez had been unable to dissuade him from informing the authorities of my presence in El Rocio. Hubert would honestly believe that he was acting in my best interests. But the story of Sanchez's involvement might have been put off for the time being. An invention. Part of the delusory cerebral activity of poor Lacey. And then perhaps Hubert had died so that he would not repeat Lacey's improbable story? His body left a good distance away from El Rocio so that it could be found almost instantly? Perhaps another story had been told by Horez—respected Dr Horez—to whom it may concern? Something about a kidnapping perhaps. I would have kidnapped Horez and Hubert in the Deux Chevaux and then murdered Hubert miles away from where he had seen me. And the Doctor had somehow escaped. Conceivable—after all, since that time I had kidnapped Hans. Why would I want to murder Hubert? Well, I seemed to be murdering people right and left.

But what about my renewed presence in El Rocio, witnessed by the congregation in the church? A sight which Horez would have been unable to predict and which had made the police resume the search in this direction? Arrangements could have been made for me to have stolen a car. Not difficult to organize. Why would I have stopped in El Rocio again? I might have got engine trougle, run out of petrol, anything. And then taken refuge in the church? To offer up a prayer to La Paloma? And fled in Hans's car?

None of it need be true. I repeated this statement to myself a number of times. The gap in the police search might have any number of reasons—such as they might have just packed up and gone to bed. There was no need to be worried about Hubert; I was the one in trouble. The police were looking for me again now; the other lot wanted me even more badly. With a groan and a sleepy grunt I switched off the light and went into another troubled sleep.

I opened my eyes in daylight. The clock's hands pointed to the time clocks have in advertisements—ten past ten. Hans was sitting on the edge of the bed about to hand me a cup of coffee he had poured out.

"Mr Lacey! You have slept well?"

"Yes," I said, realizing that he had spoken in English. I drank some coffee. My eyes were sticky, gummed up.

"I knew you instantly at El Rocio when you ran towards my car." But he seemed on edge, and not very pleased about the success of his deception. Yesterday he had been a lot more cheerful, in spite of the unpleasantness he had undergone. He continued, "Only the same day I read about you and saw your photograph in the newspaper."

That must be another picture of me. Yes, he had it to hand, on the front of some *zeitung* or other. It came off the cover of *Swallow* in its German translation.

I heard a stir over by the balcony and smelled scent. I looked over to where a girl was reclining in a cane chair with lime-coloured cushions which had been placed where the sun came in through the French window. She was slender and her face was pretty, so far as one could see around the saucer-sized dark glasses that covered most of it. They rested on her cherub cheeks and above her wide mouth which was painted in brick-coloured lipstick. It was turned down and she was in a bad temper. She spoke sharply in German; I had heard her voice the night before through the keyhole of the cupboard. A new friend for Hans—she could hardly be the Lufthansa employee he had mentioned.

"Fraulein Irma Jaegar ..." his formal introduction appeared to be an attempt to interrupt what sounded like invective.

"What is she saying?"

"She says ... she is saying I was foolish to be helping you." She had a point. He had gone to great lengths to render me his assistance—presumably even spending the night with her so that I would not be disturbed. No wonder she looked angry.

"Well, why did you help me?"

He looked very sheepish. "I was trying to explain to you yesterday ... I wanted ... I want to make some money."

I glanced at the opposite bed, where a Minolta camera with a flash lamp sat, together with a tape recorder.

"You want to interview me for a newspaper?"

He nodded.

"But you are not a reporter?"

"I am interested in journalism. Of course commerce is a more secure opening to a profession, but I believe that in due course I will become a journalist. Already I have done some freelance work. A number of my articles have been published in German newspapers."

He could make a lot of money if he handled me right. An exclusive with a man on the run. But there were risks. The Spanish police might get annoyed. He must have been frantic last night as they guarded all exits, pounded all doors. I remembered Biggs being interviewed in Argentina and recalled uneasily that the Scotland Yard detectives had not been far behind.

"Weren't you afraid of me? I had threatened you with a knife. And I am wanted for an unpleasant murder."

"Many journalists have had successful interviews with terrorists. The P.L.O., the I.R.A." And profitable. "When you said the word 'Basque' I suddenly had this idea. And then, in the car, you threw down the knife beside me and helped yourself to a cup of coffee. I was no longer afraid of you."

"You were wrong. You should have considered the danger carefully. There is a great gulf between terrorists and those who murder for private motives. Even if it is only social and not ethical."

The girl said something else with a show of irony and a pert triumphant air. I thought she understood quite a lot of English and wasn't letting on. Something about how she also thought Hans had been wrong.

"What's she saying?"

Hans looked very subdued. "She says now you will be more famous than ever."

She was holding up a newspaper with headlines the size of the top letter of an eye test. OTRO ASESINATO.

"Give me that!" The shock and disgust I felt were not reduced by the correctness of my premonition the night before.

Hans got up and brought the newspaper over to me. I glanced at the two photographs on the front. A studio portrait of Hubert; another of a corpse covered with a sheet. Even a grim piece of reporting like this came out in flowery prose. ". . . Found beyond Alamonte . . . hideous stab wound . . . miraculous escape of distinguished colleague . . . all roads must be watched . . . vigilance . . ."

The bastards . . . not Hubert. Everything I had imagined appeared to be true. Hans and the girl watched me snivel for a few minutes; she lifted her glasses on top of her straw-coloured hair, the better to observe me. She exchanged glances with Hans, who said something conciliatory to the effect that my grief appeared to be genuine. She did not seem impressed.

I poured some more coffee and tried to pull myself together. "Isn't she afraid that I might commit another murder?"

"Oh, she is armed. She would not come in here this morning

after I had told her without bringing a gun." Sensible girl. It must be in the black straw beach bag she nursed in her lap.

Hans had a one-track mind. "You will permit an interview?"

"You find me, you interview me," I muttered. "Very lucky for you. You sell a story, take my photograph. It doesn't do me any good."

"It brings you publicity. Publicity that will never be allowed to lapse."

"So?"

His English had the prim perfection you sometimes find in Teutonic linguists. "By your behaviour you have ensured that you will not be kept languishing in a Spanish prison the way your cousin was."

"What do you know about my cousin?"

"Only what I read in the papers."

I thought for a few minutes. "Order me up another meal, will you please, Hans? Not frankfurters, if you don't mind. I'm going to have a wash." I got out of bed naked. The girl took no notice; she sat in the window, eyes closed, glasses off, enjoying the sun on her shining face. There was silence while I washed and shaved and Hans read the horrible news all over again. Then he watched while I helped myself to his holiday wardrobe; I chose a pair of Levis, a yellow sports shirt and a khaki safari jacket. When my lunch came he went over and answered the knock on the door. The tray contained chicken and pineapple under a tin cover, and beer.

"Where did you get the tape recorder?" I asked as I ate.

"Irma borrowed it from someone in the discotheque. The camera is hers. She uses it on her job."

"Her job?"

"She is a hostess here at the hotel. She takes pictures of holidaymakers during the evening festivities."

"She can take pictures of me now." When Hans spoke to her she got up sulkily and aimed the Minolta at me. I was drinking beer which did not go too well with all that coffee. She had lent him the tape recorder, and now the flashlight was popping competently. She was with Hans up to a point. He was now taking shorthand notes about me.

"You will speak into the tape recorder, please?"

I puffed at the cigarette he had offered me. "I will do it when you and the Fraulein are out of the room."

"Please?"

I walked over to the French windows, opened them and looked out on to the balcony. Over the balustrade the swimming pool was far below.

"Would you and Fraulein Jaegar leave me alone? Go down and sit by the swimming pool in the far left hand corner where I can see you clearly."

She didn't like it at all. But Hans shouldn't have told me she was carrying a gun. She liked my next suggestion even less.

"Leave the camera here."

"Why?"

"As a hostage. The photographs aren't an awful lot of good in any case without some sort of statement with them."

She was the one who made the decision, and we waited, while fear, or was it her sense of public duty, combatted with greed. The heavyweight won.

"All right," Hans confirmed. "We will go down briefly while you make a statement on the machine."

She remained reluctant, and quite rightly, still wanting to wrap me up in a sheet and call in someone on the bedside telephone. And she very nearly changed her mind when I said,

"If you don't appear beside the pool within five minutes of leaving this room, I will throw the camera over the balcony. And the tape as well."

She was shrill as Hans hustled her out. I went out on to the balcony and leaned over, watching anxiously. Although the sun was shining splendidly, the March weather wasn't all that warm. The breeze blew papers about; I could see them far below, small, but as clear as the bodies round the pool. Every now and again someone dived in, breaking up the white crocodile skin patterns of light on the water. I watched swimmers gliding over the descending sweep of concrete that controlled the pool's depth. Was it heated? There were scores of holidaymakers. The majority at this time of year old and retired. Were they disappointed after making the journey from the wintry north, to find something like chill in the sunshine? Doggedly taking every advantage of their time here, they would probably not move away from the pool until the evening when they could go and watch tourists' Flamenco. And be photographed in laughing groups by Irma. They would not go near the wild life reserve. They were not encouraged to know of its existence.

To my immense relief Hans and Irma appeared and made their way to the spot I had indicated. They looked conspicuous because they were not wearing bathing suits, and Hans's skin was white and untanned. And they were quarrelling. There were no spare chairs, and they had to sit down gingerly on the concrete.

I went inside and, sitting on the bed, spoke into the recorder. I had used a similar machine on several occasions for recording bird song. Not professional recordings, but notes more or less for my own information. Now I said, "This is Robert Lacey. First I want to say that I had nothing to do with the death of Dr Moulins. He was my friend. Nor did I kill Dr Patterson. It is true that we were not on good terms, because of a professional disagreement. But I did not kill him. Nor did I witness his murder. But I was witness to another criminal episode. I saw another corpse being disposed of. The perpetrators tried to prevent me from escaping and reporting what I had seen. I believe that after that Dr Patterson was killed in mistake for me."

I switched off and went out on to the balcony again. The faces of the two below were turned upwards, her glasses very small and black. I did not acknowledge them, just let them have a good look to make sure that I was still upstairs. Then I went back inside, sat down on the cane chair and slowly drank the rest of the beer.

That brief statement was enough for Hans and Irma. It wasn't very good, and added virtually nothing to what was already known. All it really consisted of was a basic denial of guilt. Hans would have to make do with it, together with the photographs. It would be a test of his professionalism to see how quickly he could use them. He would have about half a day's start, the time it should take for me to reach the palace and organize my press conference.

Hubert had said that a number of reporters were staying at the palace. Now Hans had given me the idea of recruiting the support of the press. There was a good case for me to continue avoiding arrest and instead invoke the powers of international notoriety. Publicity might help me even if only by stirring the sleepy routines of Spanish justice. But I thought that the reporters at the palace might help me in more practical ways. Like retrieving Jaime's body out of the *cano*.

I had seen him stowed away with elaborate care. Sanchez's people had the whole of the *marismas* to dump him, but had made special efforts. He could have been thrown anywhere in the reeds and there would have been little chance of his discovery for months. He might have been laid out for the vultures and the magpies that attended them. Spring was rather a lean time for scavengers, and they could have disposed of much of Jaime, as I hoped they were dealing with the man I had killed.

Instead Jaime had been buried deep. So that he could never be found? How had he been killed? A chance encounter, a sudden quarrel? Had he been shot? Sanchez and his servants had no guns when they tried to kill me. But that was how I had escaped. Jaime had not escaped.

I remembered something else about Spanish justice. Concerned with those endless interviews involving the fate of Michael. Joaquín, helpful, conciliatory.

How long has he been in prison? Only seven months? And naturally his crime was too serious for him to get bail. But wait. What about the fellow the other day who held up the bank in Granada? He was tried and sentenced within six weeks. Ah yes, but his crime involved the military; he was dealt with by a court martial. Why so? Was it political? Was he a Freemason or a Communist or a Basque nationalist or an illegal demonstrator? Well, no, he didn't have to be. Why? Because he had shot the cashier in the shoulder.

The military dealt with all crimes that involved firearms. This was a legal custom established at the beginning of the century. Long before the civil war. You could call it an anomaly of Spanish law.

A man who murdered another with a stone or a rope committed a civil offence. He might have to wait two years or more before he was tried.

A man who shot his victim committed a military crime and was subject to court martial. That took place promptly and smoothly—he might find himself facing a firing squad over a weekend.

Had the law changed with the change in régime? I doubted it. I knew that political crime had become more widespread as increasing numbers of people found themselves subject to military discipline. The world watched as Spanish factory workers and engine drivers suddenly found themselves in the army. If the authorities wished to deal promptly with strikers, they conscripted them.

Military justice, someone once said, is like military music—just a bit different. There might be many reasons why Sanchez did not want to invite a swift investigation into his activities. He might even have an unsavoury army background.

Well, had Jaime been shot? There was only one way to find out, and that was to fish him up and see if he had a bullet in him.

But wouldn't Sanchez have got to him first? After I had been spotted in the cork tree, he would have had two tasks. One was to dispose of me—preferably to kill me, but otherwise have me locked away for a civil sort of crime like Patterson's murder. The other would be to bring Jaime up and put him in a safer hiding place—given that I was still alive and able to report what I had seen.

Sanchez must have been pleased that I was fool enough not to surrender. He knew nothing about the man I had killed on my own. He must have got to Jaime by now and redistributed him, so to speak. An operation involving grappling irons and ropes. And time. What had poor Hubert said? That the eagle's nest had hardly been left alone for a single moment? The last time they had moved Jaime about, I had been on the spot to observe them. And now the commercially minded Danes were in the same place nearly all the time, not only threatening the incubation of the remaining eagle's egg, but preventing attempts at resurrection. What about at night, when the birds were roosting and the Danes drinking? A difficult job finding the *cano* in darkness and searching with lights. There was always the odd night-time patrol in the *Estación* looking for poachers. And I seemed to remember that Sigurson was interested in night photography and the use of infra-red film. That might also interrupt underwater searches. It was quite on the cards that Jaime was still there.

I should go to the police and get them to help. If I had taken Hubert's advice on that he would still be alive. But even now I was reluctant, remembering the terrible legal paralysis that had affected Michael. When he had first been arrested he had been kept more or less incommunicado for days. Would I be able to persuade the police to act quickly? To rush over to the *cano* and check my story? I had slept for nearly a day here in this hotel. Any further delay and Jaime could be moved. And after that it would just be Sanchez's word against mine—a man of great power and local influence. Did I remember Hubert saying that he was a member of the provincial government? Or merely that he had aspirations to become one?

Of course there might not be anything to this theory. I might be totally mistaken about Spanish law—got it all wrong from Joaquín. I remembered that once, long ago, before I reached El Rocío, I planned to phone him. Should I give him a ring now? The phone was by the bed. What was his address? His apartment, all whitewash and Moorish arches, was somewhere in the *bario* of Santa Cruz, where tourists love to wander. I couldn't remember where. There were no phone books up here, and the horrible task of trying to invoke directory enquiries would involve endless delays. There had been enough delays. Soon Hans and Irma would reappear.

The best plan was to go as quickly as possible to the palace. I knew the way; I had become familiar over the last six months with the scrub and forest contained within the *Estación's* boundaries. It shouldn't take me more than three or four hours' walk. Then I could assemble the people there; in addition to the pressmen there would be my old colleagues. Not Hubert—I tried not to think about him. Miguel, though; Miguel and I had always got on. I would tell them the whole story, and then the police could move in. Would there be *guardia* standing round the palace? Very likely. I would think about that problem when I got there.

Why not ask Hans to drive me straight there? I went out on to the balcony and looked down again, wondering if his animated conversation with the girl was still disagreement. All the roads around here would be carefully watched. But I could slip into *Estación* territory direct from Matalascanas. It was not likely that the wilderness would be controlled by the police; I had been seen outside it in civilized circumstances, and they would hardly expect me to go back in voluntarily.

I took a final look round. Did I want a shot of Wasser Koln?

To brush my teeth with scarlet and white toothpaste? Hans had left Hubert's knife on the dressing table beside his non-shiny hair cream. A gesture of trust, or more likely he had forgotten it. I pocketed it before making one final sortie on to the balcony. Then, blinking from my rapid exits and entrances, I left the room for good, running along the corridor and down the stairs. It would be a little time before Hans and Irma realized that that had been my positively last appearance.

In the foyer, beside the long reception bureau, whose outer facing was covered with imitation Cordoban leather, some women were about to move off through the glass doors towards the resort's newly opened boutiques and souvenir shops. They were a good looking lot, but few organized holidays provide enough men. From the colour of their tans it was evident that they had been here for a week at least, and they seemed to have become increasingly aware of this fact. By the time we were outside two of them had struck up a conversation with me which I restricted to grunts and smiles on my side. I wouldn't be able to keep it up for long, but meanwhile the two policemen posted on the steps, observing my friendly rictus and Hans's holiday clothes, gave me no more than a glance, before turning their attention to my lovely companions. The girls were beginning to be puzzled about my lack of response to any known European language. Would I try and pass for a Yugoslav or an American? They would draw correct conclusions very soon. I peeled off from the group rather too soon to escape from the guards at the door and crossed the concrete car park. Walk slowly, confidently; look for Hans's Opel as if it were your own. It might be safer to discourage his range of movement and to ensure that neither he nor Irma was immediately mobile. Driving at high speed up and down the hotel-lined roads, they might spot me. I could use Hubert's knife and slash a tyre. But there was no sign of the car; perhaps Hans had reparked it further away in case it was recognized as the vehicle that had carried me out of El Rocio.

The group that had protected me was well on its way to the line of shops animated by hanging straw bags, postcards and Cordoba hats flapping in the breeze. I went down to the beach. Like mendacious pictures in holiday brochures it contained very few people—just the odd brown body lying low to avoid the wind. Two bathers were splashing each other—a plump man with skin burned rhododendron pink and a middle-aged woman in a frilled cap shaped like a papal crown. Some half-finished chalets, fronted by tiled pavement running into sand, bore names like Jerez, Triana, Huelva. In the distance was the battered remains of the Torre de la Higuera, a block of masonry heeled over into the sand, which had been a Moorish defence post a thousand years ago. Beside it a civil guard's station. Not that way.

The hotels fizzled out in sandy wastes and half-finished blocks of *pisos*. A crane derrick stood out against the skyline. Past an apartment block called Las Golondrinas a miniature golf-course was partly shaded by a flush of billboards advertising unbuilt houses. Then I came to an open area of weeds scattered with garbage and bisected by a road. Beyond this stretch of wasteland was the fence that followed the boundary of the reserve. Barbed wire strands were hung with a notice saying *prohibido*. Through them I could see a mass of giant heaths mixed up with pistachio thickets, broom just coming into flower, and a few pine trees. The heaths were over six feet high.

I had walked through dense xerophitic scrubland a number of times before. The animal people were enthusiastic about it because it harboured mongooses, wild boar, and in certain restricted areas, lynxes. Pigs and deer made little narrow paths that men could follow. Birds in the scrub were good too; stone curlews and night jars liked to hide in it, fiendishly difficult to see, although one could often make out their calls. Also Miguel's beautiful, stupid, azure-winged magpies; I had accompanied him through heather jungles in search of them and had returned on my own for a clutch of eggs.

A lorry with a revolving concrete mixer on its back ambled along the road this side of the fence. The first vehicle I had seen. A side road with perhaps a car every five minutes. I could sit and wait all day until nightfall, or trust to Carruther's luck and clamber over the fence now. The road was empty as I ran over the wasteland, avoiding tins and bottles, and came to the fence by one of its concrete posts. The trick of climbing barbed wire is to move with the utmost slowness and patience. It is quite possible as long as one is not disturbed. This fence, ten strands high, was more of a visual than a physical deterrent. Tourists to one side, lynxes and great bustards to the other. And the photographers who recorded the wild life on Doñana had to angle their cameras carefully so that the towers of the hotels did not become visible.

I ascended, placing hands and fingers and feet fastidiously around the strand between the barbs. Before I finished I had become rather good at the Alpine accomplishment of climbing barbed wire. At the top I had to jump a great distance down on to the sandy surface below. Just in time—an old Fiat rattled on the road behind me. Had the driver seen me? Was it slowing down? I plunged straight into an old fallow deer track that wound round and under the thick scratchy heath jungle.

In a few minutes I could sense how the air here was alive in a very different way to the smart tenements behind me. Here were rustling noises—lizards, snakes, the odd rabbit and brooding and nesting birds. Starlings, magpies (common magpies in this area) and golden orioles announced whose territory I was trespassing over. I glimpsed the bottle-shaped nest of a bee-eater built hopefully out of reach of snakes, and heard the little birds call out. Only the ticks were silent. Ticks and leeches—I gave them some thought as I brushed through the thorny sides of the deer path. They were the most obvious and visible parasites to which animals were prey. And birds too. Birds crawled with parasites which attacked every part of their bodies. A run-down passerine might suffer from fleas, feather lice, fly larvae, louse flies, mites, round-worm, flukes and tapeworms. And leeches. Miguel, with the cruelty that passes for humour in Spain, once compared the sufferings of an afflicted bird to those of General Franco on his deathbed. Horez didn't speak to him for three days.

At this particular point the scrub was not a very wide belt. It ended suddenly—a seven-foot heath behind me, and in front desolate sand vanishing to the horizon. The dunes on the Coto Doñana, lying along its forty miles of coast, are as much in content as all the dunes around the coast of England put together. Pinnacles of sand blown in from the sea move slowly over the scrub and swallow it, sliding round trees and heaths, like the ones beside me which were buried up to their waists.

In places Doñana is so like the Sahara that camels, imported here in 1829, still survive on their own. I found that where the dunes sloped upwards the sand was soft and each sinking footstep required a considerable effort, like climbing a moving staircase in reverse. The dunes kept off the wind and the sun was hot; the shivering holidaymakers at Matalascanas might envy me. Occasionally I would see marks of birds' feet on the sand's pale surface. More often I passed snakes' wave-like slitherings, and once I saw a viper undulating past in the same direction as myself like a ship on the same sea route. *Viperi Latasti* is a killer, the only dangerous animal on Doñana, or so I believed up to four days ago.

Things could have been worse. I was walking in March, before the Spanish sun caught fire. I was very hot, but not tortured by discomfort or weeping with pain. This was merely a trek on a hot English summer's day. Comparisons were blissful and I thought a lot about wading in marshes. But I craved for cold beer, and could not forget that I had abandoned the prospect of such conventional comfort. I also wished I had thought of bringing Hans's thermos.

A long walk over the sand—the sun moved about fifteen degrees—brought me to a belt of marram grass and the sea. Here was a rare sight of old Spain, a long deserted beach. I knew that this was one of the last undeveloped stretches of beach along the northern Mediterranean, running about thirty miles down the coast. Developers were also aware of the fact. Right in front of me were the haunting remains of a *casa de guardia civil* which had been burnt out in the civil war. I wished they all looked like that. Its sighting gave me an idea of my position. I wasn't far from Doñana's fresh-water lakes, Sopeton, Las Pijos, Santa Olalla and Dulce which were behind me in a line back from the sea. Their odd location has never been properly explained. Some people believe they originated as a delta arm of the Guadalquivir and then got isolated. In contrast, the actual river is so salty near its mouth that its banks are virtual desert. Not that I worried much about hydrological mysteries, but I knew that the way back to the palace was beyond the lakes.

I climbed a last mountain of sand and slithered down into a *corrale*, a grove of stone pines set in a valley of sand. It nestled at the foot of the sand mountain, and the trees along its edge were half buried. Year by year, they would sink in deeper as the sand, blown by the sea wind, gradually covered them.

I would cross this little grove in a few minutes and climb the mountain on the other side. I happened to know it well, having explored the area carefully a couple of weeks ago as a possible site for nesting short-toed eagles. Doñana can only support two pairs of short-toed eagles, which fly among *corrales* and dunes looking for snakes. They live almost entirely on snakes, swallowing them whole and regurgitating them for the chick. Only one chick, only one egg, smooth, white, short elliptical. The breeding season is late, at the end of April, and I had planned to wait for it after my expected triumph with the imperial.

This *corrale* was easy enough to cross because the stone pines grew close enough to eliminate undergrowth. I padded over the carpet of pine needles and reached the mountain on the other side which rose a hundred feet over my head. The surface sand, too hot to touch comfortably, trickled into my shoes and boiled up in my socks. Lumps as hot as lava threatened to fall on my head.

I reached the top and found myself high above the flat levels of marsh and scrub. Directly below me were two small lagoons, Dulce and Santa Olalla. These small lakes are famous as ornithological marvels. Dulce is perhaps most consistently interesting, since the fresh water attracts hoards of different species of aquatic birds. But Santa Olalla is the one that gets the publicity because it harbours one of Doñana's main attractions. I could just make out a mass of pale pink and white on the lake's shoreline. The flamingo flock moved as if a sharp breeze had puffed at sunset clouds. Between the lakes was a guard's house and behind, the flat topped woods of San Agostín resembled a raised table; beyond the woods, visible like smoke, I could see the eucalyptus that surrounded the palace.

If I went through the woods I would never reach the area near the palace before nightfall. But there was a road over to my left used by the Land Rovers. I would go down to the Tolle Erberto beside Lake Dulce, where a good path led away towards the road. Better to stick to a clear route, even if it was longer, than to try to clamber through the thickets of San Agostín. I forgot that others would reason the same way.

Tolle Erberto was a hide with slit windows, perched on stilts facing the lake. As I walked down towards it, the sound of my steps set birds moving. I had only gone a hundred yards or so when I realized that other birds far in front of me were being disturbed. A flock of jackdaws, crows and magpies were making angry conversation about another intruder. Then I saw him, walking towards the hut. A Spaniard in a shabby coat with a balaclava helmet over his head, in spite of the heat of the late afternoon. Clothes to stay out all night in. He carried binoculars. But ornithologists used binoculars, not shepherds and forestry men. He wasn't using them for the moment, and I rolled off the path into a thicket of young bracken and yellow helianthemum without his seeing me.

He went into the hut and stayed there for perhaps five minutes. Then he came out with a rifle. People who worked in the reserve carried guns for very specific purposes—like culling too large herds of wild cattle, shooting rogue boar, putting things out of their misery. This usually came later on when the marshes dried up, and the guards went round knocking off a lame deer or two which they were allowed to use for venison. Not ordinary peasants. And not in spring, the great Doñana breeding season. The only creatures to be put out of their misery at this time of year seemed to be men.

As he came out I could hear the slap and rustle of birds which had settled on the lake while he was inside; now they moved off again, scattering the lake with whites and greys of moving wings. Then to my horror I heard him saying something, adding a laugh. Someone was inside the Tolle Erberto. He had spent the last five minutes in conversation.

Had the man inside been dozing? Perhaps—the sweat on my forehead turned cold—probably he had seen me and handed the gun to the man with the balaclava who was now coming up the path towards me. He's lying there between those two stone pines. Shoot him and we'll bury him afterwards. Beneath the mud of Lake Dulce. The mud of Lake Dulce was notorious. In the summer, as the water dried up round the shore it left a quagmire that was so uncertain that it would not support the weight of a heron.

The young bracken curling around me gave no protection, and I did not dare move to try and find better cover. Hans's safari jacket had a neutral colour, but I thought that the blue of his Levis must make a conspicuous contrast to the lemon-coloured helianthemum blossoms around me. He was near enough for me to hear his gumboots squeaking on the sand. He hummed a high nasal tune which I recognized as a *saetta* I had last heard sung to a Seville Madonna during Holy Week.

The humming was interrupted by the cry of a bird. A very familiar sound—the high call of an imperial eagle. I did not dare to turn my face up to look at it tumbling, falling and circling. One only, trying a displacement technique against its prey. Undoubtedly one of the pair I had robbed—how long ago? One pair of *aquila heliaca* needs a territory of five thousand hectares or so—about a hundred square miles.

As king of Doñana, *heliaca* can be very bold. Spoonbills remain silent and immobile when an eagle alights in the midst of a colony and selects its victims at will. Miguel claimed to have seen the legendary act of a flamingo panicking when it was marked by an eagle—turning up its wings and falling to the ground, killing itself.

The man acted differently. He unslung the rifle and aimed it upwards; I could see him clearly without shifting, although I could not see the bird. The gun barrel moved as he sought to find the range. I was as horrified as if he were about to shoot me. It disturbed my tangled ethics that about one-fortieth of the world's supply of Spanish imperial eagles was about to go.

Crack! There was a shriek of aquiline rage that grew fainter as the bird soared upwards. Whether it felt fright or disdain was not possible to tell; the man had made the noise with his tongue.

"Get away you son of a whore!" he called out, shouldering the rifle again. A piece of schoolboy byplay. The bird did not return. But it had occupied him for the few moments during which he could have noticed me.

I was so relieved that I almost laughed and called out to him. But he should not have had a gun. The binoculars, which he carried by the strap without a case, thumped against his ribs. He was after bigger game. He passed by me, taking up the *saetta* where he had left off. Up the sand mountain and down to the *corrale*.

I was left alone. But not alone. Without moving I could see the Tolle Erberto and could place in my mind exactly where the slits were for the watcher to stare from. He could have been innocently watching birds. Half a dozen ornithologists could be inside, without giving me a thought. Dulce was a feeding ground for spoonbills. This was a location for the purple gallinule with its crazy purple tea-cosy body, pink head and pink legs and claws which it used like a primate's hand. If a gallinule were performing or courting, it would absorb all attention.

But the man with the gun had spoiled bird watching on Lake Dulce for the next hour or so. Rattling the door to the hide, thumping in, saving the gun, laughing, singing, he must have chased every bird away. Anyone working in the hide would have been speechless with rage at his method of approach.

Perhaps there was no one there at all? I might have imagined him speaking and laughing. I tried to remember. Could he have been merely clearing his throat? The hooded blinds of Tolle Erberto were inscrutable. If I moved, I might or might not be seen. Better not to move.

The soft sand on which I lay faced northward. The sun had not dried it up, and it was still a little damp from the rain that had fallen two days ago, that had helped me at El Rocio. There were a couple of pine trees in front of me, their silvery-green heads planted precisely on brown scaly trunks. A few yards from my nose a procession of ants made its way towards one of the trunks, carrying eggs. One was stretching itself, opening and shutting its mandibles as if it was yawning after waking up from a siesta. They walked past some pieces of broken antler partly covered with moss and lichen, which must have lain there at least eleven months. Fallow deer antlers are shed in April. Some red dragonflies zig-zagged past, and a clouded yellow butterfly chased its enlarged evening shadow. I lay, my eyes on the hide, making time pass by identifying bird calls. Too far to hear the bad-tempered voices of mallards on the lake. Here it was mostly larks and thrushes; I might as well be on Chobham Common. I heard a nightingale. Nightingales sing just as well by day, of course, but the sound suggested evening. And the light was definitely fading. The mosquitoes were beginning their evening perambulations. Beyond the lake the jackdaws quarrelled about their roosting positions as friends flew in to join them. A bat fluttered above me with that agitated silent flight, so different from any bird's.

A rustle in the undergrowth behind me. Footsteps going past, a fallow deer nearly stepping on me. He had woken from his day-time sleep and was now going to the edge of the lake to drink and then to browse. He made a good deal of noise. The wind was blowing from him to me and he passed beside the spot where I lay without the slightest idea that I was there. I could see his bright eye clearly, and the flat spreading horns that the would discard in a few weeks' time.

"Crack!" That was a sound that could be nothing but gunfire. He would never discard them now or take part in another *berrea* —the furious mating ritual of autumn. I could hear the bullet's whine, succeeded by the stag's bellow and the crash of his body.

Down below on the lake the door of the hide burst open and a figure came running round the shore and up the path. Horez ran pretty fast for an old man.

He met the man with the gun and together they walked into the undergrowth near enough above me so that I could feel the shake of their footsteps.

"Fool." They had reached the antlered corpse.

"It moved just as a man does . . ."

"I'll have to get you a permit to shoot it. Distributing guns was a dangerous error. The whole exercise has become futile. He'll be clear of Andalusia by now. Or the *guardia civil* will have him." Only futile because he had not kept a good watch himself. Distracted by birds, I wouldn't wonder, at the crucial point when I was coming down from the *corrale*. He was an authority on birds' optical faculties—good at knowing the weight of a buzzard's eye or what exactly a mallard sees when it dives after a frog. Apart from his main field of studies, which like that of so many modern naturalists, was concerned with the effects of pollution.

"Look, Doctor, look here." The voice of the man with the gun was suddenly urgent. I knew what he had seen. Up and above where the sand was soft and dry, tracks were largely indistinguishable, but here, where it was moist from shade and rain, the weary footprints of my gymshoes were clear. Going uphill, staring at the eagle, the sun shining in his eyes, he had missed them. Now he saw me. And looking around for a moment or two, they both saw me.

I was already running as the rifle spat out, and I had dodged into the trees before the third shot whistled by somewhere near my elbow. I glimpsed some lights flashing over in the direction of San Agostin. And way to the right on the dirt road a pair of headlights was turned on. Then I was in the cover of the pinewood. I remembered being in Cordoba cathedral, trying to avoid an acquaintance. Easy enough; and there were more pillars here than at Cordoba. The Cathedral, which the Moors built to simulate a forest, lacked undergrowth. The startled spit and hissing of a little owl over my head was lost in the general sounds of trying to move through bushes in the gathering darkness. But the men behind me were slowed down just as much, and the pillared structure of the pinewood ultimately made it easy for me to get a good distance away from them.

For the time being their menace had receded. But I had to get out of this *corrale* before daybreak. There were others, who would soon gather here and surround the trees, even in darkness. They would beat through here when light came.

I was going away from the lakes now, away from the direction of the palace. The wood ended suddenly in undergrowth that was impassable in darkness. Thorns and solid briar tearing at Hans's clothes. I gave up flight for a time and rested, sitting and panting as I listened. Nothing. None of the night-time sounds suggested pursuit. But I could not stay here, stuck to twigs like a shrike's larder. The moon was coming up, a more robust version of the one that had lighted me how many nights ago? It gave a faint outline to the tangle in which I had trapped myself. There was no future in going forward. I retreated in agony, step by step, back towards the forest where the trees inhibited the density of the undergrowth. It was a retreat into danger, which I made slowly and painfully.

The moon lit up a deer path, twisting in a route as irrational and nervous as the animals themselves. I followed it at an uneven pace; sometimes it was so clear that I could run at a trot; but soon it would wind away from the moonlight and I would have to feel my way along, arms outstretched like a blind man. Sometimes I wandered off it into briar, and would have to make my way painfully back.

Once again the pinewoods grew less in number. Heaths took over—giant heaths at first, which gave way to something lower, until I was walking in scrub that was not much higher than my knee. Then that all changed as I came out once again on to marshland and gazed at the *marismas* in the moonlight.

In the distance I could make out a small white square. If it had not been white the moon would not have picked it up at all. A building of some sort. Not an ordinary *choza*. What other sort of building would it be possible to find in the *marismas*? I remembered Biaggi's laboratory. I had never been to it, but that was what it had to be. And this particular stretch of water would be the *Marisma de Hinojos*. The Knee Deep Marsh. Round about 1967 an Italian called Biaggi decided that this was a good place at the right distance from the palace to build a laboratory. He made it smart, and even put in living quarters. Scientists used it from time to time. Fernando, the Peruvian, had stayed there for several weeks while he did work on the mortality of young birds in summer. Some girl students, who always got the dreary jobs, spent time here taking water samples for salinity tests. It was good for studies of horseflies and leeches.

Leeches. I could skirt around the Hinojos towards it, if I knew my way. Over there was a good chance of finding provisions. That sort of place was usually kept stocked with tins. Even the hides occasionally carried an emergency store of food. There were bunks there, provided by the generosity of the good Signor Biaggi. The hut was on a spit of land linked to the mainland by a proper path. I might eat, rest and make my way to the palace by a clear route. My pursuers would not expect me to escape again by crossing the *marismas*. Or would they? Not a wide stretch of water at that ... Less than half a mile.

The water was colder than I remembered. Better water round the knee than bullets. I bent down, scooped up some and drank a little, tasting mud. The silhouette of the hut stood out clearly now. Behind the palisade fence two wings were joined to each other, and at the angle they met was a little squat tower. The building had a positively suburban look if you could ignore the landscape around it. The beautifully constructed palings were so close together that no light was visible through them. But voices were perfectly audible.

Horsefly experts? Leech gatherers? They were talking in dialect. Friendly exchanges. Did they work for Sanchez? They might have a dog or dogs with them. If I went nearer there might be barking. Could they be squatters if they weren't scientists? Better to take no risks. I turned back in the direction I had waded. There was a light on the shore right on the edge of the water, which repeated it and enlarged it into a little yellow strip like an upside-down Spanish exclamation mark.

I went down flat on hands and knees, my fingers sinking into mud. But the moon had gone behind a cloud, and the night was now dark. If I had been an ancient Greek I might have believed that the gods that controlled the weather were rather in my favour, while others were definitely not. The man with the torch shouted to communicate with the Biaggi hut, and I listened to sleepy answers growing more alert. I heard barking—as I thought, there were dogs there. Any movement I made now towards hut or shore would involve an increased risk of being challenged by dogs and men. There was only one choice—one that I had made before.

Chapter seven

I WOULD DREAM about wading in marshes for what was left of my life. African explorers made their way through mangrove swamps for days, the smell of rotting vegetation in their nostrils. At least mangroves broke the monotony. Patterns of cloud crossed the moon as I waded on and on. Ah, here was a landmark. The sense of *déjà vu* was oppressive, as I approached the same fence dividing the reserve from the outside world that I had climbed four days ago. And after I had clambered over it for a second time, the repetitive sequence continued. I waded a lot more. The broad rectangle of a *choza* appeared against the sky. An open doorway revealed a lighted interior. Oil lamp, this time, not gas light. Dogs barked and in front of the door a figure appeared. A figure in a nightdress.

"*¿Eres tu, Javier?*" A deep throated voice competed with the dogs. The worm-ridden Alsatian cross had found me now, as I stepped on to dry land; the smaller terrier type joined him in circling round me, barking hysterically. "No, not Javier," I said as I came into the light and she could inspect my mud-stained figure.

"*Un extranjero,*" she said.

"Yes," I answered very wearily, "a foreigner."

"From the *Estación Biologica?*"

"I am Lacey." The name appeared to mean nothing to her. For an instant I even felt annoyance that my notoriety had not spread the length and breadth of the *marismas*. Then she invited me in.

I was not an attractive version of Ulysses. But Spaniards often accept the grotesque quite naturally, in the way the princess in Velasquez's picture is unconcerned about her dwarfs. The last time I was in Seville I passed time in a bar; I was the only person who took notice of the man carrying and squeezing a large plastic doll, and the deaf and dumb group quarrelling with their hands.

The interior of the *choza* was a contrast to the last one I had entered. It was spotless. The ruthlessly neat arrangement of deal furniture and the smell of bleach indicated a compulsive house-wife perpetually engaged in trying to sweep away the mud and dust of the *marismas*. The reed walls of the hut were almost entirely covered with pictures, postcards and knick-knacks in a furious attempt to civilize them.

She noticed the rust-coloured patches on my clothes and the blood pouring out of my sleeves.

"¡*Sanguijuelas!*" At once she produced salt to deal with them. A routine household task out here. As I began to unbutton my shirt with trembling hands, she said, "Wait!" and produced a bottle of *anis* adorned with a picture of Mary Magdalene on her knees in prayer. Water in a thick plastic glass turned it cloudy. I gulped down the fiery peppermint and told myself and her that I felt better. She helped deal with the leeches and ticks on my back. Three leeches lurked inside my pants which I kept on for modesty's sake until she told me to take them off so that she could wash them.

"Now?" Spanish women will joyfully wash things late in the evening, but it must have been around midnight.

"Tomorrow," she said handing me a clean white towel to cover myself. The leech bites turned it red at once. She went and found an enamel bowl and began picking up the black creatures writhing all over the mud floor. She threw them on to the remains of the wood fire which hissed. At least they had lived life to the full; I spared a thought for the millions of deprived leeches which have to go through life without a blood meal.

"I must find them all or one is sure to hitch on to the child."

"The child?" I looked at her properly for the first time. The shapeless nightdress exaggerated the matronly aspect of her figure, but she was very young, in her late teens or early twenties. She was a sleek little creature who would be stout later in life; but now her dumpiness had the endearing quality of a fledgling or a puppy. Her black hair, parted down the middle, was strained back to form the night-time pigtail that fell to her waist. In the lamplight her skin had exactly the colour and slightly shining texture of cream; it set off the regularity of her oval face and even features. Much of the time her eyes and mouth lacked expression and she looked slightly stupid unless she smiled. In animation her face was beautiful, although the bland perfection of her good looks was spoilt by a very slight cast in her left eye. A wedding ring took up half the space between the knuckles of her ring finger. "Where is your husband?" Sick? Hidden away in the curtained alcove in the corner?

"At work. He will be back at any time."

"He is late."

She hesitated. "He has been away for five days . . . he will be back at any time." She spoke innocently without a trace of fear or attempt at dissimulation.

Five days. But she must have learned about me from other sources. There was no sign that I could see of a transmitter, but I spotted the inevitable radio on the table beside the stove. She must know my story and guess that I was a murderer. She seemed unperturbed.

"I had an accident. My horse stumped and threw me and then went off before I could catch him."

She showed no signs of disbelief.

"I have been wading in the *marismas* for hours . . . I saw the light of your *choza*."

"Naturally you are one of the people who watch birds?"

"Yes."

"I worked at the *palacio* before I was married." She smiled again. The kitchen in the palace employed many girls like her. She was preparing *chorizos* for me now, with bread and bitter coffee heated up in a brown enamel jug. While I was eating she disappeared behind the curtain of the alcove. I got up quickly and went over to the battered transistor which sat between an open tin of dog food and an earthen water jar. I turned it on very low. It was tuned to a programme of sorts that whooped and died away, whooped and died away. I switched off hastily. Worn out batteries. You wouldn't listen to that noise for long. She hadn't. Not for five days at least. A silent period broken only by the twitter of a canary in a wooden cage and the chatter of a young child.

She came out now, carrying it, and put it down on a grey eiderdown. It stirred and rearranged the thumb in its mouth. She went over to a cupboard the size of a confessional and produced a pair of men's pyjamas.

They would catch up if I stayed. I should go out and go on. I felt ill, far worse than I had before Hans took me into his hotel.

The spell of luxury had ruined me. Or perhaps the ticks had something to do with it. The bites of *hyalomma excavatum* can produce symptoms like influenza.

"They will get stained," I said about the pyjamas. The leech bites were bleeding merrily. She shrugged. A few raspberry marks among the stripes were a challenge to her washing prowess. The pyjamas were for a smaller man than I, and fitted tight as a torero's outfit. She opened the curtain to the alcove and revealed the matrimonial bed. Dour ironwork framed newly made-up sheets and a thin blanket. She and the child must have been sleeping here when I arrived. I didn't ask where she would sleep now.

Trembling I pulled the sheet up. Many things conspired to keep me awake—the bitterness of the coffee, all the small pains in my body, the whine of mosquitoes and faint speculation about my pursuers. But I slept and the thought of grey men pushing out over the marshes only came in dreams and did not wake me. I was only woken after daybreak by a little girl with gold studs in her ears who was standing beside me beating me over the head with a wooden spoon.

"No," I said firmly before I was fully awake.

Her eyes were very large. She backed away, smiling and waving, not saying a word, like the queen mother. After she disappeared I could hear her chortle to herself. There was no sign of her mother. Outside washing no doubt. I pulled myself up and sat on the edge of the bed. Clothes had been laid out for me belonging to the same frame that fitted the pyjamas. I dressed stiffly. The leech wounds had closed up. Crablike, I slid through the curtains. Like most *chozas* the place was windowless but one of its two big doors was open so that a big rhomboid-shaped piece of sunlight lit a patch of the floor and the edge of the glass-topped sideboard that sat so incongruously in front of the reed walls. I made my way towards the light and stepped outside. She was not washing clothes but sitting on a stool milking a thin cow. She wore a black polo-necked sweater and tartan trousers tucked into gumboots. The child, who was squatting beside her probing the sand with her spoon, also wore gumboots, small scarlet ones.

She sat humming the unforgettable chorus of the grisly song which won the European song contest for Spain all those years ago . . . La, la la, la. The sun, glistening on the surrounding *marismas*, emphasized the barren isolation of the island that made up her home. Its sandy surface, covered with closely cropped grass, was raised for about half an acre above the surrounding water. The area, which would increase in size as summer came, supported geese, dogs, hens, puppies and a goat. Far off another cow and a more than usually miserable horse had given up the struggle of finding grazing in the vicinity of the *choza*, and were wading in the sedge-spotted water.

The *choza*, surrounded by a broken palisade and bits of recently strung wire, ineffectually designed to keep the child from drowning, looked very African by daylight. There was a little more vegetation than appeared at first glance, for around the back a hedge of prickly pear guarded a plot of beans which was wired off minutely with fine mesh wire. The stretch of mud before the hut, where she sat easing milk into an orange plastic bucket, was strewn with piles of very old, mostly broken artifacts —buckets with holes in them, wash tubs, a wooden ladder, a spade, an axe, home-made clothes-pegs and bottles. Her fanatical sense of housekeeping did not extend outside her front door. Everything here looked as if it had been washed up and left behind by flood waters.

"You must be very lonely here," I said.

She stopped singing and looked up at me with surprise. "This place is not so isolated. Especially now that summer is coming and the water will dry up. In summer we go once a month to El Rocio."

"How far away is that?"

"Seven kilometres."

"Is that the only time that you see people?"

"No." She laughed and pointed. "We have neighbours." I spun around in alarm at the direction of her finger. Over on the horizon I could see another *choza* looming out of the water like an ark.

"Do they come to see you often?"

"When the water goes down."

"Will they come today?"

"No. The water went down a little last night, but it will be a month or more before it is gone." Along with clouds and sun she

134

noticed the level each morning. *Marismas* stay away from my door.

"How do you get away from here in winter?"

"What need is there to get away? We have what we need here. We get most of our supplies before the rain comes in October."

"Has the child ever been sick?"

For the first time she looked troubled. "When she was a small baby she had fever. My husband had to take me in the boat to El Rocio. Then I got the bus to Seville to the hospital where she was born. She was well after that."

"The boat?"

"Yes, that boat." It lay among the debris, small and flat-bottomed.

"Do you have oars for it?"

"Oars? What use are oars in the *marismas*? No, the horse drags it."

I remembered that regular transport across the marsh was often provided by a horse's tail. The passenger sat in a boat and held on while the horse pulled him along. One of the most primitive means of transport in existence. In Ireland the conquering English felt that the custom of ploughing by the tail was proof of the barbarity of the native Celts.

"That horse?" It stood sadly far out from the island, knee deep in water.

"Usually my husband's horse. That one—that is the one I ride when I go to El Rocio."

"How do you catch it?"

"My husband catches it with his own horse."

"Doesn't it stray?"

"It is hobbled. It can go quite far. But never out of sight."

"When does your husband return? Today?"

"I do not know." The frown on her forehead deepened. Last night she had been afraid of me. Now of him. But her courtesy prevented her from telling me to leave quickly before he appeared. Giving the cow a slap so that it trotted off, she seized the child by the hand and waited, carrying the bucket in the other hand, for me to go before her through the portals of her front door which were constructed out of raggedly cut tree trunks. I turned and caught her troubled eyes gazing at me as

I limped into the dark interior of her home. Its neatness struck me again after seeing the desolate exterior. Perhaps the outside was considered the province of her husband. He could have little time to take care of it, if these weekly sojourns away at work were a regular feature of his routine. There seemed to be little trace of his presence inside. A shaving mirror on the sideboard and clothes in the cupboard. And a little portion of belongings in a corner—a tool box, an old guitar and some magazines about bull fighting.

She cooked *desayuno* for all of us—coffee and bread for the adults and warmed milk for the child, to which she added pieces of chocolate from a packet stamped with a picture of the Virgin of Cabeza. The Virgin and Mary Magdalene are familiar trade marks in Spain, like the Bisto kids. While she worked, heating up the little stove, blowing the charcoal aglow, taking the coffee out of a sack, I wandered round restlessly peering at the exhibits carefully taped and nailed on the thin parallels of the reed walls. There were a lot of postcards: balconies covered with geraniums, whitewashed churches, curves of seacoast, corkscrewing toreadors. Interspersed among them were photographs, mainly formal. Someone dead, lying with hands folded and eyes closed; an old man. Stiff wedding groups, the child at its christening. Some smiling snapshots taken at a beach rimmed with hotels. Certificates indicating attendance at shrines throughout Spain: La Cabeza, the Sanctuary of Tiscar, El Rocio, little pictures of the Virgins who reigned at these places. Several of La Paloma *in situ* above the altar as I had seen her, or outside the church in the midst of a crowd of pilgrims. A calendar with a bunch of grapes and two sherry glasses. I examined several more solid decorations—a pair of castanets and a doll in white satin and lace which appeared to have been garrotted with fine wire in order to hold her upright. Hanging nearby was a little shillelagh painted over with sprigs of shamrock. On its blunt end was written MADE IN JAPAN.

"Where did you get this?" I asked.

She glanced up from the pan she was stirring. "At the *romerio* at El Rocio. It is a *recuerdo*."

"It is a *recuerdo* of my country."

"What is your country?"

"Irlanda."

"Ollanda?"

"Irlanda."

"Ollanda." She became animated. She knew all about the land of efficiency and monster cows. Her sister had gone to work there and had brought back tales of thick rich cream and the good life. She herself had chosen to remain at home. She had a job which she loved at the palace. Again I remembered the laughter and singing and good nature that perpetually emanated from the kitchen. Yes, I could imagine her there. She, it seemed, could imagine me there.

"You are like so many of the people who say at the *palacio*. Some"—she was too polite to mention who—"think that you are all locos. Wasting all their good money looking at birds."

"Birds are the most beautiful of God's creatures," I said sententiously, my style of speaking influenced by all the purse-lipped goddesses staring at me out of the pictures on the wall. A hen tripped in at the doorway and ruffled its feathers in the sun.

"Birds are beautiful when they are in the pot. Were you out watching them last night? *Lechuzas? Chotacabras? Mochuelos?*" Lovely words, finer than Latin or English for owls and nightjars tried to veil the curiosity which she considered a breach of courtesy.

I limped to a bentwood chair and sat down. "Yesterday afternoon," I said,—I owed her a lie at least—"I was riding through the *marismas* towards the Algaida."

"What in the Virgin's name does anyone want to go there for?"

"To see *cigueñas*." She raised her eyes to her forehead in exaggerated amazement. I wondered what the staff in the palace made of real fanatics like Patterson and Hubert. "I was watching, um ... *milanos y buitres*. The horse stumbled. I could not catch it when I fell in the water and it trotted on." The tale of Johnny Head-in-Air taking a tumble was accepted in silence. It left a lot unexplained. Why had I not waded back towards the palace, forever looming on the horizon? Why had I bothered to cross the wire out of the *Estación* when it made such an unmistakable boundary? I might have had to waste time making myself more convincing, but there was an interruption. Just as I prepared to lift my coffee to my mouth, I heard a sharp explosion and the cup dissolved in a shower of white splinters and liquid all over my bread, which lay drowned on its plate. I looked up, dripping, as the child watched me, smiling, having shattered my breakfast with a well-aimed pebble.

I yelled at her mother.

"Ah naughty little Carmelita . . ." Discipline was administered with a couple of playful taps. They were only to impress the ill-natured foreigner, but they made Carmelita scream and roar until she was rewarded with a sweet from a screw-top jar, which was kept on a specially constructed bracket shelf nailed uneasily to the reeds out of her reach. It was ungrateful, I knew, considering how I had been welcomed and who I was, and her mother's loneliness offered special pleading, but as I watched her cram the sweet into her mouth, fluttering her black eyes at me, I was consumed by a cold northern hatred of children. All over the Mediterranean and throughout Arabia they are indulged and spoilt, but it seemed to me at this moment that outside Spain they absorb such treatment. An Arab child has an inherent dignity and self-sufficiency that the posturing and pouting Spanish infant lacks.

"How old is she?"

"Nearly three, Señor."

I wondered how well she could talk and what she might tell her daddy.

The incident had one result; it made our relationship more relaxed. A bit of honest shouting was part of the normal atmosphere of this household, and perhaps my hostess was used to something more in the nature of domestic disagreement. I had recognized the formal face of her husband in the wedding photo on the wall; he was cleaned up, but he had a distinctive Roman nose. The charcoal burner. I sipped a new mug of coffee and crumbled fresh *tostado*. I must get away.

"What is the best way for me to leave this place?"

"You must go the way you came . . . or," she hesitated . . . "you could seek help from the *chozas* over there . . ." She pointed through the open door.

"Who lives there?"

"Two families. They are good friends to me. One of the men works on the same estate as my husband. Their places are very modern. They have Butane stoves and Rosita has a television which is run on a battery. Also they have a car . . ."

"A car?"

"In winter it is put up on bricks. In summer it can be driven on the hard mud. Rosita, she can go where she pleases when summer comes . . . her husband is good to her . . ."

I said again, "It must be lonely for you," and this time tears appeared in her eyes. "Many women living in the *marismas* are lonely. They have been so since the days of Doña Ana." I knew about Doña Ana, the lady who gave her name to the region in the sixteenth century; wife of the seventh Duke of Medina Sidonia, she had been a recluse. "I have Carmelita for company."

I took a guess at what was bothering her. "If I go over to your neighbours they will guess that I have spent time here, and they will tell your husband . . ." She carefully wiped a speck of food from the corner of the child's mouth. I noticed a ragged scar on her left earlobe beneath her earring, which looked as if the ring had once been torn off. "Perhaps he might be rough with you." He might beat her to a pulp. In fact I had no intention of going over to the *chozas*; some of the people there, at least one a workmate of the charcoal burner, were connected with Don Sanchez.

She was crying, and that made the child cry. Several minutes of wailing and petting ensued.

"You should have turned me away last night."

She sniffed back some tears. "I know what it is like to be trapped in the water . . . Look . . ." She got up and went over to one of the doorposts on which a pencil mark made a line about eighteen inches from the ground. "Three years ago . . . before the child came. I was *encinta* . . . The floods during the spring rains . . . this high . . . I had to wade through water up to here" —her hand hovered flat near her stomach—"to seek help at the other *veta* . . . How could I turn you away?"

"I must leave." The unspeakable marshes spread all round to the horizon. "Do the dogs always bark when people are approaching?"

"They can hear my husband when he is over a kilometre away . . . he whistles and they reply. I know that he is coming long before I can see him." There wasn't a stir out of them.

"Could I catch your horse and use it?"

She looked doubtful. "My husband always rides out on his own horse like a cowboy. He has a rope."

"If . . . if I could catch it and ride away, what would you say to him about it being missing?"

She thought. "I would say that he had strayed."

"Has he ever strayed before?"

"He can always do it for a first time. The hobble could come loose. But first you must catch him. I do not see how you can do this?"

"Have you any oats?"

"Oats?"

"*Si, avenas.*"

"No, why should we waste money on *avenas* for the horse? He is eating grass out there."

"Have you anything that it might like to eat?"

She went off and rummaged in a brown cardboard box, and found three fluffy old carrots. I could only try.

Again I was limping through marsh water. The horse stood still and far off in the windless air, a painted horse upon a painted ocean. He remained immobile for a quarter of an hour until I had waded to within twenty feet of him and then the lifted his head and splashed off with an indignant whinny. He settled himself at a distance and watched and waited, as I slowly approached a second time. The hobble didn't seem to be much use and I felt similarly handicapped. I made encouraging noises; there was no way of conveying to him the feast that I carried. He moved off again.

Did he seem a little less reluctant? I was getting nervous, because we were getting within dog's ear shot of the other *chozas*. Shaking my bowl of rotten vegetables, I wondered if I dared venture any further . . . and then suddenly as I approached the horse once more he stopped and let me catch up. His look of depression was ludicrous—a cartoon horse with an underslung lower lip and drooping eyes. What happened to his legs and hooves—did they become spongey? Not noticeably, I decided after I had slipped the rope halter over his head and bent down to remove the hobble. He munched away at the carrots. One fell into the water and he nosedived after it like a heron. He was thin and undernourished. One thing to take the girl to El Rocio, another to support my twelve-stone weight—where?

He followed meekly when I led him back towards the *choza*. I felt euphoric. I forgot my terrible stiffness and ran knee high, not for terror, but for joy. I leaned down and tossed water in the air so that it caught the sunlight.

She had been watching from the break in the palisade. She had been there for some of the time at least, because I had noted her plump little figure during my splashing and searching.

The horse and I came in almost at a trot. Once he had surrendered he showed enthusiasm or at least resignation towards his proper role and moved willingly enough. He had become more animated and had half lost the look that he was going to cross his legs and fall down in the water. I brought him on to the land and tied him to a piece of fencing. She was watching me, smiling.

I should have gone at once. Then and there I should have arranged the bits of blanket, rag, leather and rope that made up the horse's crude saddle. I should have splashed off, leaving her safe. But Nausicaa had changed her role and become Calypso.

Both the front and back doors of the *choza* were open, creating a through draught and a passage which the chickens used as a runway. The high-pitched reed roof allowed a cathedral coolness inside the hut, insulating it against the midday sun. Later in the year the layers of reed would be unable to keep the summer heat at bay. Now the spring afternoon lacked the heavy drowsiness of later siestas.

To celebrate the capture of the horse she found another bottle of *anis*, and we drank a good deal of it, smoking the cigarettes that had survived a rough passage in Hans's safari jacket. Meanwhile the child had to be fed and then persuaded to lie down for her siesta nap. Even with the aid of sweets this took a very long time—time for an odd courtship, prolonged by Carmelita's wails and punctuated by *anis*. I grew impatient—but not because I shouldn't be lingering here during the hot noonday hours. Perhaps the island nature of this place gave a false reassurance; it had a fortress feeling. Instead of thinking of escape and pursuit, I began to recall details of the de Maupassant story where a lover pinches his mistress's child black and blue in order to get her undivided attention. Carmelita was put to bed, refusing to be comforted by sugar lumps, peppermints or a kitten. But in due course her angry wails subsided and the only sound in the afternoon was the canary singing.

Carmelita's mother giggled as I kissed her neck, hidden away by black hair and black sweater. It was not easy to get to anything else as I found, undoing all the little pearl buttons on her shoulder before tearing the sweater off. Underneath were more complications; she was parcelled up in underwear, some of it pinned with a holy medal. There was a scent about her, something like Lifebuoy; she was as polished and scrubbed as her primitive little home. She had dark feathers protruding from under her arms, and I began to understand why continental men consider this feral and sexy. If I liked the hair on her head would cover them. Her bun was made up in plaits; I took out the barley sugar pins that held them up and unrolled the bands at the pigtails. I tumbled the straight white parting that cut her skull in two. The hair came down and hid the top of her tartan trousers, and now she took those off too. They were Black Watch. A sonsie lass. I carried her over to the matrimonial bed. She was light as a cat.

Mosquitoes circled like predatory birds, and their humming was a perpetual accompaniment. I slapped one dead on her white shoulder, and took my hand from her breast to claw at another. Later we forgot about them.

"What is your name?" I asked as the patch of light in the doorway changed shape.

"Asunción" she murmured. She didn't ask me mine. Later she went over to shift the canary out of the sun and fetch the cigarettes and what was left of the *anis*. "Where did you learn to speak Spanish?"

"I lived for some years near Granada with my father and my cousin. A long time ago."

"You've only been there? And here?"

"And up in the Sierra de Cazorla where they have another great game park like Doñana. And in Galicia where wolves are still to be found."

"When I was a little girl my father killed a wolf. I am glad there are no more here now." In summer wolves might have given an added dimension of terror to her isolation. "Where else?"

"Over in Teneriffe."

"What were you doing in Teneriffe?"

"Looking at *vencejos*."

"Though you are a fine man, you are mad. You have never

gone to those big places on the seaside? To Malaga or Tossa del Mar?"

"No."

"Never been to Malaga! A foreigner and you have never been there." The legend that Malaga, Tossa, Torremolinos and Benidorm are heaven upon earth is as widespread in provincial Spain as it is in British travel agencies.

Talking brought back some reality. "I must go."

"Not yet." When the sun had shifted away altogether the child woke and began to whimper. She got up and dressed quickly before going over to comfort her. She changed her nappy and gave her tostado and milk, singing a gentle song called 'Pajarillo'. Pajarillo means little bird. I held back the curtains of the alcove to watch her. While she was singing, the dogs began to bark.

I was naked. She put down the child, which began yelling, and rushed over with my own clothes. All clean and immaculately smoothed by a charcoal-heated flat-iron. When had she found time to do that? I dressed in a panic and rushed outside to dress up the old horse.

Voices carried over the water and movements were just visible far off. I looked, badly missing my binoculars, and thought I could make out some horsemen.

"You stayed too long," she said, taking on another Greek role. She was Cassandra now, as she helped me mount.

"Do you never ride with estribos?" I asked irritably. My horsemanship would be tested as I jogged along stirrupless on an old blanket tied to the horse's skinny midriff with the aid of a wide leather girth.

"My husband has the good saddle." I had seen him using it when he was burying Jaime in the cano. Now it was coming, no doubt, over the water.

She took the horse and led him round to the other side of the veta so that at least the bulk of the choza lay between me and them. She handed me up one of the many pieces of bleached wood that lay around the little island. We did not speak as I gathered up the ropes that were substitutes for reins. I thought that the dogs' barking was growing more frenzied.

Once after I rode off I looked back at her. She had her head on one side and was plaiting her hair in frantic haste.

I needed the piece of wood every step of the way. I banged

the horse's bony haunches to persuade him into a trot which I had to endure banging up and down on his spine. Behind me there did not seem to be any human voices above the dogs'. I had a little start.

The horse was obstinately making for the second *veta* which I had avoided earlier in the day. Every time I tried to head him off he veered back. The bridle was little better than a halter, the two ends of the rope merely tying up on the noseband. It seemed to communicate little sense of direction. I belted the beast again, and he moved with an action that was like trotting in treacle. Then I thought that it might be a good thing to go straight across the *veta* ahead, rather than try to avoid its system of reeds. Dogs were now barking ahead. Beneath thin eucalyptus trees showing against the dark sky, *chozas* similar to Asunción's loomed in the dusk. One of them was already lit up with the familiar greenish gas light. As the dogs gathered round, the horse hesitated, almost throwing me. I dug my heels through the blanket and hit him as hard as I could. There were people running about. This was a proper community without any true sense of isolation. Asunción's carefully maintained loneliness might satisfy some medieval lust for possession on the part of her husband. Otherwise it seemed extraordinary that no one had visited her for a week. I thought they might be afraid of him and suddenly felt very frightened for her.

The figures I glimpsed in the dusk seemed old or feminine. Voices were querulous. There was someone witchlike in black, a younger woman in trousers who could have been Rosita, and a great many shrill children. Someone was throwing stones and all were shouting at the tops of their voices. Did they think I would stop? I realized that their shouts were not directed at me. They were calling over the water towards Asunción's *choza*.

There was a thick belt of phragnites reeds which I had to avoid by riding round the *veta*. Dogs continued to yelp at the horse's hooves, and out on the water I could hear an accompaniment of frogs. The horse baulked when I put it to him that we were entering the marsh again, but he responded to blows, and we were soon out in the water. Then I heard a new sound which I took to be an unusual sort of frog croak, until I realized that it was a wheeze coming from his lungs. I slowed him down and listened again. The cries behind me were more distinct.

"Hoy, hoy, this way."

"This way!"

It was dark now—lingering with Asunción had given me that advantage. I wondered what sort of story she was telling. She had assumed that I intended to avoid her neighbours. I had no desire to meet them. We were betrayed by her horse.

I had him at a walk now, and he plodded through the water with scarcely a splash. He was on a loose rein, and for all I knew might conduct me in a huge circle back to where he came from.

The mass of stars gave an outline to the horizon. The night reflection seemed much less of a true mirror image than the serene repetitions that appeared in the calmness of day. The sedge and tufts of grass appearing above the water's surface mingled with the reflected stars like black holes. The horse moved on slowly, sometimes putting his head down and snatching at a piece of invisible green stuff. He wheezed continually, a little escape of sound from his windpipe like gas. Once he became excited when a herd of wild horses made a lot of splashing and neighing in the darkness. He made some effort to catch up before the noises receded and he lapsed into his own stumbling gait. He walked on all night. The physical effort of clinging to the barrel of his trunk with my aching knees and calf muscles kept me occupied much of the time. A lifetime of custom might allow shepherds and cowboys to guide their animals without stirrups, and I was not going to emulate them with much success during one spring night. But the eight inches or so between my feet and the water was the difference between heaven and hell. Although the back of the horse was not comfortable, it kept me from wading. It occurred to me that the old man in the first *choza* might have had a horse—otherwise his movements from his home would have been even more restricted. I had gone off in a panic without looking round. I hoped very much that if such an animal existed it was not shut up in a stable.

I dozed for a time, falling into the state of accustomed relaxation that is supposed to overtake troopers on campaign. Troopers had stirrups; I nearly toppled into the water. I nearly did it four times. Then a big red sun shot up and shone in my eyes.

It was the second dawn in which I found myself faced with a view of the marshes all round me. The scene was surrealistic. Dali

145

had first painted in Spain and had been familiar with queer breathless landscapes like this one. Or was it more properly a seascape? The horse had stopped moving. The bull standing knee deep in water glaring at us with the sun over its shoulder might have posed along with one of Dali's melted watches. He was the familiar figure on bullfight posters, the model for souvenirs with his rectangular body, generous haunch and massive shoulders; the velvet bag of his scrotum swung above the water. Except that being a wild bull of the *marismas*, he was reddish brown instead of black. He was about to charge; his tail flickered and he adjusted his head for a better aim. I was reminded of a photograph of Impulsivo, the bull that nearly killed El Cordobes. The horns were thin and sharp—*astifinos* was the correct term. Bulls would charge if an intruder was on what they considered was their territory. Or if they were courting. Or if they felt contrary.

As he swept by the horse pecked and changed pace to a hysterical side step. But the bull had passed us and did not turn round; he galloped off with a speed that I envied. The horse continued to play up, his terrified movements accompanied by a shrill neighing that alternated with his wheeze. Then he bolted, if the sombre splashing movements he made could be so described. I was prepared for this, but taken by surprise when, from wading up to his knees, he suddenly dropped down—and the water was playing round his withers. I should have held on to the blankets and rope as he steadied himself and began swimming. But I didn't. Horse and I came adrift, and I watched him floating away, the rope reins trailing in the water and the blanket ballooning out behind. Then he heaved and plunged, working away with his forefeet. With a tremendous effort he regained shallow water once again and was trotting off as fast as he could, far faster than I ever imagined he could move. His rope reins trailing in the water reminded me of Patterson's half-tamed falcon blown away by the storm.

The story I had told Asunción was re-enacted, as I found myself drowning in a substance like chocolate *mousse*. I had to swim a bit to stay alive before I felt a bank under water and found a shrub of glasswort that had a worthwhile root. Like the horse I could pull myself up so that I had the privilege of once again standing in water, with the prospect of having to wade some more. All was explained; the bull had charged because it had felt itself on the defensive with its back to deep water. Another *cano* whose location the horse had misjudged in its fright. It might even be a submerged stream, which would only reveal itself when the rest of the *marismas* dried up.

After I had finished swearing, my first thought was that Asunción's washing was ruined. Then I saw that land was not far off. Wading would be minimal, for just ahead of me was the line of reeds I had seen before when I approached the Isla Major. I was near the Brazo de la Torre. Not at the same location—here it was miles down stream from the rice plantations. I had come around the *marismas* and their surroundings in a great weaving circle.

When I reached the banks of the Brazo de la Torre I was only just able to find some dry mud. The long line of the reeds was watery, and the bank almost submerged except for a narrow sloppy path on top. I could almost keep my feet dry. A similar line of mud marked the opposite bank, and beyond was more water. Upstream or down? Upstream would get me back to the rice-growing area in due course, but going that way could easily put me in touch once again with the Conde and his friends. Downstream the Brazo de la Torre joined the Guadalquivir. If I went that way I would find some sort of ferry on the river bank and across to San Lucar de Barremeda or to Bonanza. I would approach civilization from there, away from the lethal wilderness of Doñana.

I walked downstream, a thick belt of reeds on my left growing in a long line that followed the river's straight course. As I strode along I began to notice the inevitable traces of man the despoiler. The reeds contained large numbers of empty cartridge boxes that had not sunk through into water. They were mostly containers for twelve-bore ammunition used for killing duck or geese ... I picked out well known brand names like La Marca or Celta and the manufacturing marks of Union Explosivos Rio Tinto S.A. Many of the boxes looked fresh. They had not been left lying around, one assumed, by legitimate hunters, since shooting birds was supposed to be forbidden for the time being. The fraternity of poachers must be very crowded; here they had been taking advantage of the banks of the river, a good place for marksmen who had no boats.

Then I began to see dead birds. One has got used to rubbish everywhere, and for a time I mistook them for pieces of rag or plastic or paper. So many of them were black or white—egrets or coots. Too many of them. Caught in the reeds. When I realized what they were, I first assumed that they had been shot by hunters and their corpses abandoned as worthless. But in a few minutes I had passed several dozen, some not even dead, but gasping out their lives. Some were waterlogged and others were caught in the reeds like paper kites that had made accidental landings.

The reeds were full of nests, which was one of the reasons why this place attracted poachers. One of the pleasures in wandering among reed beds is the frequency with which you come across nests anchored safely above the water. (Although I felt that it would be a long time before I did any wading for pleasure again.) On the Estación nests like these would be protected, but out here they were regularly robbed and the eggs eaten or sold. Not this year, however. I saw a couple of mallard nests with the mothers still sitting, quite dead. Dead coots . . . seven, eight, nine, fourteen, fifteen . . . I have a particular affection for coots which are intelligent birds. When a coot's nest is threatened with flooding, the whole family will help to shore it up. If coots live near traffic they will sometimes learn to look left and right before crossing a road.

I picked up the corpse of a little squacco heron that had got its long legs and neck entangled in reeds. No obvious signs of emaciation. Full adult plumage. Later in the year, of course, death among young birds was an expected occurrence. The drying up of the *marismas* resulted in an unpleasant annual harvest of death. But it was part of the harsh rule nature imposed on the place. This was different because it was unnatural.

I had been in constant contact with corpses recently, but the massacre I now saw disturbed me at least as much. Naturalists are misanthropes, more upset by the loss of the *Torrey Canyon* than the loss of the *Titanic*. I counted numbers of dead squaccos —their deaths would be more important ecologically than that of coots and mallards. But the menace to other species nesting on Doñana was obvious.

Could this be a repetition of the bird destruction that occurred in Doñana a few years ago? Nineteen seventy-three was it, when fifty thousand birds had died. Eighty per cent of the spoonbill population had been wiped out, and herons, coots, storks, plovers and wild duck had all been affected. At that time it had been feared that the death toll would increase with the arrival of migrating birds from northern Europe. Detonators managed to divert a good many newcomers away from the poisoned areas to safe places where food and water was provided. Something of the sort might have to be done now, before it was too late.

Ornithologists had been baffled by the symptoms that caused the mass death. Originally chlorate pesticides had been suspected, but further investigation by a couple of Dutch scientists showed the main cause to be botulism, a bacterial poison which flourishes in hot dry conditions.

I began to wonder if I ought to collect evidence for a report, but reflected that others would soon see this devastation. I tried to estimate how great an area the infection covered. I counted dead species for a time, and then gave up wearily. The initial unpleasantness of the muddy half-flooded path where I trod was compounded by this visual torture. It was an enormous relief to turn my attention to the vista of the Guadalquivir. At its mouth it has a grandeur that it lacks further up above Seville, where it flows through marmalade orange groves. Down here there was something Amazonian about the proportions of *el gran rey de Andalucia*. Where the Brazo de la Torre poured into it, the width from one bank to the other was a good half mile. Bank was scarcely the description of what happened this side, where nearly everything was covered with flood water. But the brown mainstream of the great muddy river was as distinctly separate from the marsh as if it were composed of a different substance.

No proper river bank meant no houses or villages, just continued mud and water. I had not expected anything very much in the way of settlements on this side, but I had pictured some sort of place where I could hire a boat to take me over. I could see boats. Out on the river. Small rowboats bobbing up and down a few hundred yards away. They were tiny, and every now and then they seemed to vanish under the waves that the wind blew up. I thought each time that one had finally gone under, but it would suddenly reappear. They seemed to be making slow progress towards a spot in the middle of the river where I could just make out a line of nets. I realized that they must be sturgeon nets. At the palace, during the sessions in which we regaled each other with horror stories about pollution, someone usually brought up the case of the sturgeon fishers. Pollution had virtually killed off the sturgeon in the Guadalquivir, but the fishermen refused to admit it. They continued to set out their nets during the time of the spring run when the fish were supposed to come up the river to lay their eggs. With luck they might catch one or two, or even half a dozen in the course of three months spring fishing. Some seasons they never saw a sturgeon at all. And still they continued to try, year after year—like this little convoy out in midstream, satisfying itself that there was nothing in the nets but weeds and brushwood. I roared at it and waved my arms, but the boats were all far away and well out of earshot. They were going with tremendous effort against the tide back to the far side of the river where civilization beckoned.

One thing was dismally apparent. I would have to spend another night out in the wastes. I had underestimated the wide expanses of the Guadalquivir, had wrongly imagined that I would find a string of villages attended by boats popping backwards and forwards over the river. Instead there was the continued flood, and I was trapped in it for some time longer.

On this bank there seemed to be no sign, except for the poisoned birds, that man had set his foot here. That was not quite true. Downstream I could make out a couple of buildings and a broken-down pier. Around this little complex were some corrugations where the ground had been drained. I could see a small tower like a church belfry, some pieces of machinery, and a boat pulled up on the mud. I watched it for some time as I splashed towards it, but there was no sign of life.

It took me the best part of the afternoon to get anywhere near the place. A passage that continued to be littered with corpses tangled in reeds. The sun was hot, the water round my feet, sometimes lapping over my ankles, was warm. I felt dizzy. The dead birds in the waterscape began to seem a natural feature.

Coming on to land again was like stepping into another dimension. For so long the world had been covered with water. Now I reached a long straight sandy stretch of territory that was immune to flooding. Around the buildings was a series of earthworks raised a few feet above the water in neat squares. They were enclosed by a broken-down fence adorned with an official notice nailed to a post which said PROHIBIDO AL PASAR. An iron gate tied with a piece of twisted wire made no real effort to keep out intruders. Against whom could all this derelict protection be? Thieves rowing over in boats, landing from helicopters? For what? For salt, it seemed. There were some tanks which turned out to be disused saltpans, at the bottom of which were old encrustations of salt packed in layers like squares of ice. Littered around them were piles of rusty machinery. A crumpled track had taken wagons down to the collapsed pier, perhaps with the aid of the broken winch. There was a boat beside the pier which gave me a surge of hope. But it turned out to be nothing more than a cage of rotting ribs.

The two houses beside the *salinas* had the same air of desolation, and it never occurred to me that someone might be living there. I changed my mind when I saw the cat. It sneaked out from beneath some girders and watched me with amber eyes, looking sleek and well fed. Could it be making a good living on local rats? But the hens wouldn't be doing that. They began to appear one by one, leggy creatures, running about pecking at invisible titbits with the air of simple-minded happiness that condemns all battery systems.

The main house with its bell-tower and two closed windows was very dilapidated. I peered through cobwebby glass into a dark interior. There was someone there. Lying in bed, propped up against a bolster, so immobile that at first I thought she was dead. Another woman on her own. I moved away from the window, and with the extra sensitivity of the sick she must have noticed something or perceived a change in light.

"Enrique, is that you?"

Enrique could not be far off. I looked down river, and there he was, coming this way on a horse. He had a rifle slung across his shoulder. I could declare myself to him, go back into the *marismas* again, or try to hide among the other buildings in the *salinas*. Unlike Asunción he would most likely recognize me as the man wanted for murder. But I was on my way to give myself up in any case. There was no good reason why I should fear asking his hospitality, and the chances were that he would give me a hot meal. If only he had a boat, so that our acquaintance could be reasonably brief. The gun put me off. I suddenly realized that I might be walking on land owned by Don Sanchez. If this stretch of the river belonged to him, there was a good chance that the people who lived on it might behave disagreeably. Better to hide from that lonely man and his gun.

I examined the second house in the *salinas*. It really was unoccupied. I established this after circling it cautiously. One room was used for the hens, and a little hut had been converted into a stable. But there were several other rooms which seemed to be used for storage. The door of one was ajar. I stepped inside among coils of rope, sheets of plastic and tins.

If there had been a dog I would have been discovered at once. But these people were unusual and only possessed a cat. I manoeuvred about until I found a chink in the wooden wall through which I could watch the man approaching. He dismounted and immediately, without going in to see the woman on her bed, began to do the chores. He threw a handful of grain to the hens before shutting them up, calling the stragglers in increasingly abusive tones until he slammed the door on the last one. He went inside the house for a moment and came out with two plastic buckets. He filled them at a pump, one for the horse and one for use inside. He led the horse to its little stable and stayed with it for some time, feeding and watering it. When he finally went inside his own house, I could hear the woman's voice quavering.

"You were a long time, Enrique . . ." I could not hear his reply, but she was moaning, "I feel bad, very bad . . ."

I looked around the storeroom. The rope seemed new and I didn't think the stacked tins on the shelf had been there for long. Nearly all of them contained an insecticide; their sides had similar bands of yellow and red, and the words PROPTEX–H in red lettering across the side. Many of them had been opened, emptied and tossed into a corner. The remains of a white chalky substance was visible at the bottom of some of them. I wished passionately that they might have contained something to eat. Then I noticed down on a lower shelf a box of bleached wood containing some other tins whose size and shape suggested food. They had lost their labels, and were a little rusty, as if, perhaps, they had been washed overboard from a cargo vessel. Paint? No, paint tins never looked like that. When I tried to think of all the non-edible things that might be contained in tins that shape, my mind kept reverting to things to eat. Tuna fish? Sardines—no, they had traditionally shaped containers. But what about mackerel? Meat —processed pork, stewed Argentine beef, casseroled beef frankfurters? Rice pudding, or was that essentially an Anglo-Saxon nutrient? Olives—I had seen them put in tins like that. Shrimps, instant *tapas*. More likely tinned fruit. Don't let it be tinned fruit, I muttered, using Hubert's knife. A jet of red liquid like blood squirted in my face; I was not prepared for skinless tomatoes. The let-down would have been total if I had not been thirsty as well as hungry. They slipped down my throat, cold as oysters. Insubstantial too, although I told myself that a certain amount of flour went into their preparation. Was there any point in opening another tin? They might be a mixed lot. Out squirted red juice again. I persisted; they all contained tomatoes.

I had to make the choice of going and knocking up Enrique or trying to forget about my hunger. In the end I stayed where I was and dossed down on coils of rope and sheets of plastic. I hoped passionately that this would be the last night I would sleep out. I would change the ropes I was lying on for forty years on a prison mattress. Or for a coffin. But I managed to sleep until the cock woke me. He crowed from his hut to indicate that sun was coming up over the Guadalquivir. I staggered outside to face another terrible morning with a half beard, filthy rumpled clothes, a sore throat, incipient arthritis, diarrhoea and hunger.

I thought of robbing the kitchen, but imagined that the invalid would be insomniac and would hear me. Then I had an idea, and approached the hen house which was kept shut by string and a bit of wood. I opened it, letting the hens stream out like factory workers after night shift. Enrique would know immediately that someone had freed them. They had not had much time to lay— I was afraid that they would not have laid at all, since I had heard no triumphant cackles, only the thin cry of the cock. But the blessed ladies had done their work quietly, had laid four eggs that spring morning. I ate them raw, feeling a sense of irony as I handled them with as much reverence as anything laid by *aquila heliaca*.

I wondered if I would risk using the pump, and decided that I must. It was situated inconveniently far from the tower house for domestic purposes, which was to my benefit. It squeaked. To hell with it. I pumped away, drank my fill and put my head under the rush of water. The cat came running up to investigate, purring its tail held vertical. But Enrique and his sick wife continued to sleep or, at least, be silent.

The *marismas* had sharpened to a tail, squeezed out on one side by the river, on the other by trees. I could avoid the water altogether if I walked inland for a bit and hit the river again further south. The trees were stone pines, part of a *corrale* set beside sand dunes. The sensation of walking on dry land was luxurious, and the ease of passage in the warm early morning sun was marked by flowers. I came to a glade full of coarse grass and cistus. Cistus loses its petals after midday, but now it displayed circus colours. I lay and rested in a bower of garish pink and yellow, looking back to the *salinas* far away on the horizon. But I should have moved more rapidly. I continued to underestimate the extent of acreage dominated by Doñana.

The pines made shade under which it was easy enough to walk, unless they had thinned out so that the vegetation beneath them became correspondingly thick. There were open glades with more cistus and the occasional tracery of paths. I lost my direction half a dozen times. Twice I came upon small circular pools of silver ash which indicated a charcoal burner had been at work. Later I came upon his hut. It was shaped like an igloo, except that instead of snow, there was straw thatched on a wooden frame which curved to the ground. No window, only a minute opening down near the ground. Inside a man must have just been able to stand up. The dark straw made perfect camouflage so that I blundered right up to it without seeing it. A dog, tied to a stack of faggots, barked and pulled on his rope until he nearly choked. For a moment I wondered if the owner could be Asunción's husband, Don Sanchez's servant. When I heard a gravelly voice calling out, asking itself and the dog what the matter was, I backed away, losing myself in the undergrowth.

Beyond the *corrale* I climbed a hill—not a hill exactly, but a bow-shaped sand dune solid as many a mountain. On the top was an obelisk, one of the white markers known in Spanish as *trigos*, indicating that the importance of this hill was in relation to its incomparable view. I paused to read the notice warning off vandals and trespassers. *"Instituto Geographica—vertice geodisco —la destrucción de este semal penado por la ley."* Such proof of enlightenment through technology combined with law seemed as out of place here as the hotel towers of Matalascanas. But I could see civilization from beside the *trigo*. I looked across what remained of Doñana and over the Guadalquivir. There was a final segment of *marismas* and then a long line of trees to the river's edge. On the far bank, houses gleamed through the haze; I could make out the port of Bonanza with its lighthouses and lines of anchored ships. Over there was the grim safety and unpromising future that I had tried to reject before. Doñana had defeated me.

An hour's struggle down the hill skirting the *marismas* brought me to gaze on the same sluggish flow I had met upstream. The river banks here were marked at regular intervals with small wooden projections pushed out like abortive piers, probably as a means to stop erosion. Across the water Bonanza seemed very near; I could see a proper pier, festooned with fishing boats, a large white building like a palace or a monastery and a lot of small houses that gleamed as if they had just been coated with spring whitewash. Even more bright and glittering were some small triangular white mountains situated upstream from the pier that glistened and twinkled like ice and snow. I puzzled over them before concluding that they must be piles of salt from a properly working *salinas*—nothing like the miserable ruin I had encountered on the Doñana side. Over there I could sense activity; this side had only desolation.

But somewhere on this bank there must be someone with a boat. Even if no organized ferry service existed, there must be communities with fishing boats and rowboats such as I could see out in the river. Two fishing boats chugged by in mid channel, and a prawn boat, its net held on two poles behind the stern, drifted slowly past. As I sat on the bank a few moments longer before gathering myself to continue walking, I became conscious of the sound of louder engines. A big vessel was coming down river from Seville, chugging along my side of the bank. A whistle sounded over the trees and the sun caught the white bulwarks of a large cargo ship; a red funnel came alongside and the gradually emerging hull, topped by two lifeboats on derricks. Then I caught sight of the Red Ensign.

It was not sensible to assume for one second that she would stop and pick up a stranded tourist. Even the spectacle of another murder wouldn't have been enough to make the captain switch off the engines and heave to. But I shouted and waved my arms. Three men in white overalls leaned over the rails and gazed at me. The oldest was a chiefy or engineer type who smoked a pipe as if he was advertising it in *Country Life*; the other two were listening to his waffle with a pleasantly abstracted look. Then they caught sight of me dancing up and down. They began making faces and Churchillian gestures with their fingers. Their faint cat-calls, just audible over the noise of the engines, wafted back to me over her stern, over her pretentious name, *Valiant Endeavour*. I stood and cursed all the citizens of Swansea, which, according to the writing on her backside, was her home port.

Chapter eight

THIS STRETCH OF bank was along a water highway—fine for estimating cargo tonnage to Seville or for watching all the different sorts of ocean-going vessels that could accommodate themselves to the restrictions of the river. But there was no sign of any sort of ferry. I hoped very much that there might be fishing villages further downstream on the final estuary where the Guadalquivir met the sea. Somewhere there must be communication with the opposite bank.

I estimated that the shortest way downstream was to leave the river bank once again in order to avoid another patch of marsh. But the scrub in which I found myself was thick as jungle, an almost impenetrable growth of decayed trees and bushes. Gradually the going improved until I could walk easily with few interruptions apart from the rustle of a snake or lizard, or the whirring of partridges flying from under my gym shoes. It took miles and hours to rejoin the river. A few herons flew off at my approach. The soft mud along the bank had been churned up by the snouts of wild boar seeking roots. I caught sight of a tusker feeding away, half as big again as a domestic pig. The books say they are nocturnal creatures, but here he was, snuffling and snorting at midday. He became aware of my presence, and after looking me over with his angry little eyes, scuttled away into the undergrowth.

The Guadalquivir was as slow-moving as ever, just the same as I had seen it bearing away the *Valiant Endeavour*. Perhaps the sweep of water was a little more chocolate-coloured than it had been upstream. Bonanza looked exactly the same. My depression increased as I stared across at the same steamers anchored before the white town, the same sparkling pyramids of salt beside the mud flats. But I had got just a little nearer to human contact. I found a pier, a proper nautical construction with a beacon nearby, striped like a barber's pole in bands of red and white. It was freshly painted, and a coil of new rope lay beside it.

A well-trodden path led downstream. As I walked along I remembered from my researches that Alexandre Dumas had sailed this part of the river in 1845, noting the banks "crowded with wild fowl, ducks, bustards and gulls almost as large as eagles." Lucky old Dumas to be in a boat. There were no bustards now, but I noticed hundreds of waders. Nothing wrong with them at all. The pollution or pesticide upstream had done them no damage; it seemed to be confined to a relatively restricted area, and perhaps, if it did not spread, the devastation of a few years before might be avoided.

Intent on watching birds, I stumbled upon the village compound, a group of *chozas* totally African in spirit. I would not have been surprised to see negroes with spears and drums. A dozen huts were set on rolling sand dunes with stone pines towering above their steep roofs. Each had its own little garden and briar or cactus fence, and its decorations of geraniums in tins. Geraniums did not suggest Africa. Nor did the two old ladies sitting outside a *choza* trying to shade their eyes from the afternoon sun as they sewed. The only thing black about them was their clothes. An old man was bent over a plot of land planting out young tomatoes. Down on the little spit of sand overlooking the river there was no sign of boats.

Dogs brought the children to life, and they all came running over to inspect me. Their elders regarded me more leisurely.

"Who are you?" croaked one old lady.

"I am a foreigner. From the *Estación Biologica*. I had an accident in the *marismas*."

She was deaf, and this had to be repeated by the other old lady with the incomprehensible dialect.

"An accident? He looks as if he had had an accident."

I remembered that I had money, and said what was now uppermost in my mind.

"I am hungry."

"You have permission to be here, senor?" asked the deaf lady. "All this land is *reservado*."

"I have permission," I lied, and then bellowed again, "I am hungry."

"He is hungry," shouted the non-deaf lady.

"I am sure he is, if he has had an accident. No food in the *marismas*."

"I have money. I will pay for food."

"He has money."

"Juanita," the deaf lady said, "go and get something." A small girl disappeared inside the *choza*. I squatted down beside granny's chair. The old man had given up planting tomatoes and came and stood near. "It has been a good day," he said.

"I want a boat," I told him. "To hire one." I was too abrupt. I should have wasted some time in earnest courtesies.

"A boat señor? What do you want a boat for?"

"I want to get to Bonanza."

"You wish to cross the river, señor?"

"Yes, to Bonanza. I wish very much to go to Bonanza."

"You will need to find someone who will hire you a boat, señor."

I took a breath. "Yes. Would it be possible to find someone who will row me across the river?"

The non-deaf lady interrupted. "Do not pay any attention to him, señor. There are no boats. All the men are away fishing." She pointed in the direction of the Guadalquivir and the open sea.

"When do they return in the evening?"

"After sundown. They will want to rest. They will not go to Bonanza in darkness."

"Is there anywhere here where I could find a bed for the night? I would pay."

"Stay the night? Here? No, señor."

I watched a large cargo vessel chug upstream in the direction of Seville. "Why?"

"At nightfall the men return. Every *choza* is then filled."

Conversation lapsed for a time. The small boys grew closer, staring and pointing. Like Africans, I thought again. Preserved in their kraals, part of the colourful scene, owned by some rich huntsman. Less entertaining than the wild boars, but part of an old conservation scheme. The continuance of a medieval way of life such as this was considered a most desirable *status quo* by many experts.

The little girl came out of the *choza* carrying a thick white china plate loaded with slices of dark oval bread. A tin of sardines, the top just curled back to reveal one beheaded body.

An orange. Pungent cheese. She went back inside, and I started to wolf food.

"How did you have your accident, señor?" I did not answer, because I was concentrating on prising a sardine out of the tin with my fingers. The girl reappeared carrying a bottle of mineral water. *Revoltosa.* Never mind. I took a swig to wash down some bread and cheese.

A woman came out of one of the other *chozas* with a slop bucket whose contents she emptied on geraniums. She was in black with black heelless slippers. She was the first person I had seen in that community who was over ten years of age and under seventy. She spotted me from a distance, walked over a few paces and said,

"That is the foreign murderer they are looking for."

She said it loud enough for both the old ladies to hear. The reaction was operatic. Young and old started to hiss *asesino*. I ignored them and continued eating, even when two boys picked up stones. "Carmen! Maria! Dolores!" Other plump figures in black appeared from other houses. I had finished the plate quicker than a dog eats its dinner, and was now drinking more mineral water and unpeeling the orange. I might have brazened it out. There was no man in the village.

A line of mules appeared out of the forest carrying sacks of charcoal and bundles of rosemary which they were going to deposit down on the sand beside the water. Sooner or later a boat would arrive and carry them over to Bonanza. But not me. The mules were led by three brawny men who did not belong to the village, but were friends, I gathered from the shouting, lisping exchanges. Just three men turned the crowd into a mob; I got up and ran before all the explanations were made. The scrub under the pines made good cover so that within minutes I found myself alone except for some dogs. The shrill women's voices died away, and it was impossible to tell if the men had taken up the pursuit. But the boys were running after me. I could hear them moving lightly and not very fast—bare feet had to blunder over sticks and thorns. The dogs kept catching up and I'd throw things at them, making them retreat for a moment with a howl. Looking back I'd catch a glimpse of a head covered with curly black hair or a tattered red shirt.

How many were there? The eldest could not be older than

eleven or twelve or he would be out at work. Why weren't they at school? No school here. I longed for a school master ... someone respectable, a priest, a shopkeeper ... a *guardia civil*. I was a more interesting quarry than rabbits and birds. Wild boar and deer were forbidden game in a reserve like this, which would be subject to a set of medieval hunting laws. What was I to do? Hurt them? In guerilla armies all over the world small boys have made efficient soldiers. I felt very much how I would dislike being killed by one.

I came out on to the beach beside the river once again. There was the usual wide Guadalquivir and open sea ahead, scattered with tantalizing fishing boats and a long oil tanker fighting against the river current. Along the bank I found I had reached a proper beach which was bounded by a sandy road with tyre tracks on it. Looking at them I felt like Crusoe spotting the footprint. There was a notice, COTO PRIVADO DE CAZA, and I could see a grove of eucalyptus trees ahead.

I ran down the sand, the absurd hunt distantly behind me, a few dogs keeping up, nuisances like flies round the face. I got up to the eucalyptus and found that I had come to the heart of the large feudal estate through which I had been blundering for the last two days. *Chozas* were scattered on the sand dunes, but there was much more. A two-storey building with a red-tiled roof as substantial as the Palacio de Doñana loomed behind walls and a massive gateway whose pillars were topped with stone pineapples. The big wooden gates were open so that I could see lines of green shutters along the building's whitewashed walls. Outside on the sand was a gibbet made up of five wooden poles supporting a long cross-section from which hung the carcases of three deer. Beyond them was a handsome stone water-trough and a couple of chained bollards.

Behind me the first of the barefoot boys had emerged from the wood and was running along the sand. Another lot of women and children materialized from the *chozas*. The gates between the formal pillars were closing now; gates in Spain never stay open for long. They had only been open to let out two men on horseback. One was instantly familiar. Here he was again, I noted without surprise; not a charcoal burner really, merely a man who neglected to wash. The other was dressed formally for riding, with leather chaps, tight buttoned-up short jacket and wide-brimmed sloping grey hat. He carried a gun. He turned his head and I saw a great bruise down the left side of his face, red and mottled against his suntan. I guessed that he might have got that when I gave him a whack with a spade in the rice factory at El Rocio.

Both men spotted me as I stood trying to regain my breath. There was nowhere left to run. A third man, an old fellow on foot, who had bolted down half the gate, also saw me and suspended gate closing for the time being. The man with the gun drew it slowly from its saddle holster—a good hunting rifle, I thought, perhaps a .45 Parker Hales. He held it under his arm and pointed it at me casually, flicking the barrel with a couple of little movements towards the half-opened gate. That was the way I was to go.

The watching crowd was silent, except for the odd murmur and a sudden furious row as some of the dogs which had followed me embarked on a fight. Silence fell again as I walked through the half-opened gate, the horsemen following behind. The old man inside slammed the other half of the gate shut.

I waited in front of a formal Renaissance garden while the horsemen dismounted. Little, low, coloured flowers were planted in patterns crossed by box hedges. A double hornbeam hedge, the arms of each tree stretched and bound on wires, led towards a double flight of steps and double doors topped with a pediment and a stone-crested shield. Elsewhere were outbuildings, servants' quarters and a private chapel. The man with the gun nudged me round to the back, past a group of palm trees whose boles waved in the evening breeze. Through a door into a dank corridor with a sudsy smell of washed flagstones that had not dried. The air hummed with the distant throb of a generator. In the kitchen on the left, down two steps, a woman, scraping mussels out of their shells, did not look up as we passed. I caught a brief glimpse of a table scattered with chopped onions and the navy blue shells with their bright orange contents. The corridor turned at right angles and ended at a baize door. No, it did not end; behind the door the quality of life was improved by a line of antlers and a jute runner. Also dozens of photographs, very similar to those at the *Estación*, showing groups in brown sepia standing behind stags, birds and pigs laid out in rows. Many of them were dominated by the pale foxy face of

Alfonso XIII exuding a dignity that turned his pixie hat into a crown.

We stopped in front of a photo of his white steam yacht anchored in the Guadalquivir and a plaque commemorating a royal visit in March 1908.

"What shall we do with him?"

"Find Julio. Move on, *hombre*." For all his appearance, the charcoal burner was the one who spoke with the voice of authority.

The corridor debouched into a hall whose walls were lined with groups of stuffed animals and birds. Lynxes prowled in glass cases. One case, standing upright, contained a great bustard, the first I had seen on Doñana. An old man in a dark coat was standing beside some bee eaters whose stomachs were pierced with wire. In his hand he held a long feather duster. It seemed late for housework. But he was not dusting, only swatting bats; one had been slapped against a rare blank patch of wall and left a stain before it slithered twitching to the floor.

"Who is this?"

"It's him."

"Where did you get him?"

"He walked in the gate."

"How?"

"I am telling you. Twenty men searching the *marismas*, and he has to come down here and walk in the gate."

"Don Sanchez must be informed."

"How? How are you going to reach him?"

"He went up river to the *salinas*. Enrique sent word that someone had been there last night." Several people must have gone up and down beside the river. But the wilderness area was so vast that I had seen no trace of them.

"When will he be back?"

"Who knows? Presumably to dine. There is no hurry now this one is caught."

Don Sanchez would scarcely plan to eat before ten o'clock. It was just on dusk now – the butler was pushing down bulbous brass switches, and dim lights from a chandelier composed of sweetheart pink and blue glass made the eyes of the stuffed birds shine.

"Take him upstairs. The usual room. The door will be locked, but the key is in it." As we moved the charcoal burner muttered something and took the Parker Hales from his companion. We went up a main staircase, lined with more photographs; if I could have paused I might have counted every single partridge killed by King Alfonso and his friends. There were other pictures too, some modern, sportsmen posing with their rifles aimed, dogs retrieving ducks. The sepia changed to black and white and the photographs got increasingly arty. One sequence taken with a zoom lens showed a cornered boar ripping up hounds.

At the top of the stairs corridors led off between lines of bedrooms. This was another palace that had been built to accommodate huge hunting parties. A hairy arm reached around and opened a door. The grim little bedroom smelled of damp; all buildings in the *marismas*, however imposing, are damp. In the fireplace a pleated piece of black paper was balanced on some mildewed newsprint. The Moorish cupboard was genuine, and very different in its imposing bulk from the imitation at the hotel. A single narrow bed spread with white pique had a curved, black, japanned head painted with flowers. Underneath I glimpsed a blue and white chamber pot with a pastoral design.

"*Hombre,* turn round."

I hadn't quite turned, so that the first blow of the rifle butt hit me under the ear. A slightly different aim might have knocked me out, but this just threw me to the floor. The second blow was on my jaw; teeth were loosened. I felt I had to spit or choke, and I rolled over on my stomach, so intent on spewing out blood and saliva that for a moment I scarcely felt the blows running down my spine. They are all cruel here, I thought, and remembered how I had once seen a group of boys outside a Galician village tormenting a swallow. They had it on a long string, and every time it flew off they let it get quite far before giving a tug and pulling it in hand over hand like a kite. I screamed and turned over on my back again so that I could look at the charcoal burner striking away methodically. He was Asunción's husband. His companion enjoyed himself giving some feeble aid—an occasional thrust at a knee or a forearm with his boots. I had suffocated his friend in a mountain of rice. Then my collar bone broke or snapped out of position, something like that, and I fainted. When I came to the butler was standing there with some rope in his hands.

"You won't be needing this," he said, and they laughed.

They went off, the man in the smart clothes wiping blood-stains off his leather chaps with a handkerchief. I was left lying on the floor. It was not self-respect that made me drag myself to my feet and make for the bed. Over the past week a bed, a proper bed, had come to symbolize for me the utmost in luxury. This was probably the last time I would ever rest, and it seemed typical of my orgy of bad luck that the mattress on which I arranged myself was uncomfortable. There was a crackling of horsehair and I could feel buttons. The pillow smelt mouldy. I dribbled blood on to the pique and thought of Asunción imprisoned on a lonely island in the middle of the marshes. And yet not too remote for a seducer. I lay unable to doze. The knobs of my spine gave off pain like a row of gas jets.

Later Horez was standing over me and the light was on. The butler stood beside him holding a libation in a pottery bowl painted with blue and white patterns beloved by tourists. He set it down on the chair beside the bed and I saw it contained something like milk. Watered disinfectant. Horez proceeded to patch me up a little. I remembered him boasting how he was thrice a doctor—once a doctor of medicine and once a doctor of biology as a result of his paper on the effects of lead poisoning from stray cartridge shot on different species of water birds. And the University of Grenoble had awarded him an honorary degree.

He set my collar bone competently. "I'd have thought," I said gasping, "that your medicine might be a bit rusty." He was an old man and had been studying *gavidae* and *ardeidae* for thirty years.

"I was a field surgeon in the war." He meant the civil war, of course.

"Which side?" I asked to take my mind off the pain.

"The side destined by God to conquer." He squirted some penicillin into me. They have a special reverance for penicillin, like holy water. I could not believe that its long-term effects meant that I was not going to be killed soon. He was making a medical gesture.

"Could I have something to ease the pain?"

"No."

Amazingly I could walk. I'd probably suffered no more than

a steeple-chase jockey who'd had a nasty fall. The doctor took me out of the bedroom, leaving the butler to tidy up. For a minute we were alone together, and I suddenly wondered if I had anything like the strength to kick him hard and try and make a run for it. The temptation was removed instantly since the charcoal burner and his companion were waiting at the head of the staircase.

Lights were dim and shutters drawn over all the windows hid the outdoors. Even so I felt that the time was late at night. It was cold. Don Sanchez waited for me in a large salon thicketed with antlers. They embraced numerous armchairs, were entwined around lampstands, and one was even twisted around a large barometer. Others patterned the walls in rows like feather stitching between further batches of group photographs. There were a few conventional chairs, a leather-covered sofa and small tables. On either side of the fireplace hung pairs of crossed spears, eight-foot long bamboos with evil-looking blades for sticking pigs. Silver-mounted boar's tusks ingeniously held them in place. One wall had been cleared of antlers and other clutter to accommodate a large scale map of Doñana covered with flags and pieces of tape. In front of a rosemary-scented fire lay two dogs —a labrador and a springer, conventional sporting breeds. A console table covered with drinks was situated under a still life of disembowelled hares. I noticed some sherry decanters that looked like old Waterford glass, and for a moment mused on the Irish connection. I remembered hearing that Don Sanchez had acquired this place through his wife; she had been the one with the conventional background, sherry interests, aristocratic relatives and Irish ancestors.

There were a number of men in the big room, but I only noticed plump Don Sanchez, waving his hand to the butler, who poured him out a glass of Seagram's whiskey. He was in hunting clothes as usual, wearing the jodhpurs we had jeered at and a jacket of such a complicated check that from a distance it resembled chintz. He had on round thin-rimmed glasses and he was looking at the map.

"¡Venaqui!" He had not given me a glance, but there was no doubt whom he meant. As I approached he backed away a little.

The *plano topografico* covered the whole of the Doñana area, a triangle bounded on one side by the Guadalquivir. The wedge of land owned by Don Sanchez was very small in comparison to that belonging to the *Estación Biologica*. At one time the estate connected to this grandiose palace must have been much larger. I tried to recall some more of Hubert's gossip. The wife's family had been troublesome. Her brothers out of Spain during the thirties, up on the Riviera, gambling and living it up. A lot of land sold; Doña Sanchez hadn't brought her thrusting husband much of a dowry. Not that he needed it; before her death he had done well enough on his own.

The tape on the map, held with black pins, began somewhere near the site of the cork tree, reached to Villafranco and turned back to El Rocio and Matalascanas. Three independent blue pins were placed at Dulce, at the old *salinas* beside the river, and a spot in the *marismas* not far from the Brazo de la Torre which I knew must be Asunción's *choza*. My route had been carefully studied.

"Is it correct?"

"Yes."

"What happened at Villafranco? What happened to Salvador?"

I would rather not have talked about the poor devil in the rice. They must have got a clear account of what happened from the man who survived. When I hesitated, Sanchez shouted,

"Give his arm a shake."

The charcoal burner was behind me. Only a little nudge was necessary. Who needed truth drugs or special interrogation techniques? Now they were questioning me about the time I spent in El Rocio. They were not interested in my conversation with Hubert. Naturally, since it had been monitored by Horez. Only in the German tourist. The charcoal burner had seen him, and so had another man who mumbled from the back of the salon. He didn't move around much, since he was on crutches. The back tyre of Hans's Opel had made a mess of his foot.

I needed no pressure to talk about Hans. "I persuaded him to take me to Matalascanas." There was the nitty gritty. Sanchez might behave like a warlord on Doñana. But not in the civilized skyscrapered haven for sun-worshippers. "He was interested in my story. He was a freelance journalist. You must know that my disappearance has become an international sensation."

"Perhaps," Horez shrugged. I had the satisfaction of seeing that he had turned white as a Falangist uniform. "I have noticed a few foreign reporters staying at the *palacio*. They need to titillate their readers. An English reporter from the *Sunday People* tried to interview me. That is a Socialist paper? I am happy to say that the Spanish have chosen to ignore your adventures..."

Spanish newspapers don't usually have much to say except about bullfights, football games and the hairstyles of Princess Caroline of Monaco. But my story had not been subject to censorship.

I said, "I had the opportunity of reading a good deal about myself in the Spanish press."

Horez conceded the point, adding, "But your claim to have had contact with a foreign reporter cannot be true. Any interview would have been published before now."

"I made a tape recording," I said, and added a lie. "I arranged for a delay in its publication." I wished now that I had. I could have taken the tape and posted it to Hans, to any address he cared to give me, even back to the hotel. The story would have been delayed, so that I could still have given it fresh to the reporters at the palace. And yet, it would have been in existence if things went wrong. But I had been unnaturally optimistic, believing that things couldn't go on going wrong.

The silence lasted a little time. More Seagram's was poured out. The company lounging behind us shifted restlessly. A pine cone spat in the fire.

"What did you say on this tape?"

My lies were an exercise in wishful thinking. "I gave an eye-witness account of the disposal of Jaime's body which I saw through binoculars. The presence of...him...Sanchez. My deduction that the man had been shot, which made his murder a military crime. You don't want the military involved."

"You thought that out?" Sanchez muttered, and Horez added, "Why did you not give yourself up and tell your story to the *guardia civil* and get them to seek for...the evidence?"

I held up my free hand and opened the fingers. "Five dead men." Was that correct? "Sorry." I move my thumb across the palm. "Four." No need to mention the man I killed at the *choza* if no one had heard about him. He was irrelevant to this discussion. "I was already assumed to be responsible for the death of Dr Patterson. I thought that if my theory was correct about the bullet in Jaime's body, I would have to act very quickly. If I allowed myself to be arrested, there would be inevitable delays. Questions. An appearance before the magistrate. Difficulties in persuading the police to drag the *cano* at once. I thought Jaime would come to the surface quickly if I went direct to the palace. Get assistance from the reporters and other people there. I had already wasted time in the hotel in Matalascanas. Sleeping. I thought I could get to the palace in half a day from there. But your people made that impossible."

"What else did you say on the tape?"

"What else? Nothing?"

"Sure?"

"Nothing, I tell you. Nothing." They gave my arm another shove. What else did they want to know? About the man I killed? Asunción?

Horez was saying, "I do not think he could have known."

Sanchez's voice was raised to a shout. "Before he went to Villafranco he must have hit the Brazo de la Torre. He could have seen the experiment from there."

"Not possible. It began well downstream from Villafranco. And he was only at the *salinas* afterwards."

"Ask him. The rest we can deal with."

"Before you reached Villafranco you were on the Brazo de la Torre?"

"Yes."

"Did you notice anything?"

I looked bewildered.

Horez said, "He hasn't made the connection. And you must realize that others are bound to go along the Brazo de la Torre. It always has poachers, especially at this time of year. Inevitably there will be reports."

Reports on what? I remembered suddenly. "Dead birds." And I made the connection with the *salinas*. Tins. Tins and dead birds. Tins stored in the wooden sheds at the *salinas*. PROPTEX –H. Red writing on white labels. A pesticide. Rather a lot of pesticide.

Acres of marsh along the Brazo de la Torre covered with dead birds.

The last time there had been a pollutive killing of birds on the Coto and scientists had made enquiries about its origins, the rice people in the area had vigorously denied accusations about the over-use of pesticides. They had been justified when the bird mortality was attributed in due course to botulism.

But supposing that epidemic had given Sanchez and his associates an idea? To organize a more extensive slaughter of birds? There was a particular chemical compound in insecticides that could poison on a wide scale. My brain faltered and then remembered.

"Carbopenothion." A bad word to say aloud.

If those tins were used in concentrated form, it would only take one or two to destroy the flamingo colony, for instance.

But why? Horez and Sanchez were in whispered consultation and I was guessing again. Proptex-H used deliberately in bulk would cause irreparable harm to the bird population of the *Estacion Biologica.* When all those birds died on the last occasion a number of scientists had expressed much-publicized despairing convictions that any more similar massacres would mean the end of the reserve.

If there were another major disaster at Doñana on a truly vast scale, which destroyed migration patterns and killed off whole species, the future of the *Estación* would be in jeopardy. The World Wild Life Fund and the Spanish government would be realistic. Cut their losses. The place would be put out of business ornithologically. And Don Sanchez would acquire the poisoned land. *Marismas,* perfect for converting to rice fields. Long beaches, fit for dozens of hotels.

"It seems a ruthless way to expand commercially."

Horez understood my silent deductions. Horez, an international authority on pollution, the man Don Sanchez came to consult so frequently at the palace, bringing his hunting house parties along as camouflage. Horez had made the same ornithological betrayal that I had, and I was hardly the man to condemn him. But he attempted to justify himself to me. "In Brazil as much virgin forest is destroyed each year as could cover the whole of the Guadalquivir delta. Pollution will kill off these birds in due course. We all know that in our hearts. This plan was merely a speeding up of the process."

I said, "The results of carbopenothion poisoning along the Brazo de la Torre were insignificant. A stretch of two or three kilometres, not even on *Estación* land."

"What you saw was a trial run. We had initial doubts about the effectiveness of the chemical. Unfortunately the guard, Jaime, witnessed our activities and planned some blackmail. There was an argument. Later, of course, we will spread the insecticide on a far wider scale."

"Later?"

"We plan a time when those who live in this part of the Guadalquivir delta are absent from their homes."

I guessed. "At Pentecost?" The *romerio* at El Rocio would be attended by rich and poor from all over the region. Dukes, peasants, shopkeepers, making their way across the parched countryside to acknowledge the Little Dove. She would have their undivided attention.

"But you could not hope that pollution the way you plan it would pass as accidental?"

"No." Horez did not seem perturbed. Pentecost was at the beginning of the hot weather, a time when there was a high mortality among birds in any event. The devastation in seventy-three was not noticed at first because of the natural death toll. That could happen again; people at the *Estación* might easily be slow to realize what was happening. Most likely they would initially attribute the deaths to another outbreak of botulism. And even when they traced them to pesticides, deliberate pollution would be the devil to prove in law. And the birds would be dead.

But there were snags now. Publicity had been directed towards the area. Whatever Horez's optimism, I should have thought that the ambitious plan involving Proptex-H and slaughter would be a washout. Even if it were assumed that I was responsible for all the human deaths. One thing at a time. Later, implications of my interference with the great scheme could be discussed at leisure.

"Is that everything?" asked Sanchez.

"I think so." The fire had died down but still glowed pleasantly.

"What do you want done?" The voice of the charcoal burner behind me.

Horez gave patient instructions. "His body will have to be found. There must be no question about identity or about the fact that he died accidentally. The best thing would be for him to be drowned."

171

"How? Throw him into the river?"

"There is never any guarantee that a corpse in the river will reappear." No Mediterranean tide to throw it back. "He will have to be discovered in the *marismas*. Near the *palacio*. Somewhere along a route frequented by bird watchers. A patch of water that will be drying up over the next couple of weeks—so that he will come to notice. One of the smaller lakes, perhaps."

"You wish us to take him to the *Estación* and kill him there?"

"No, kill him here first. Much easier. You can drown him in the bath."

Sanchez had reservations. He said that a post mortem might suggest discrepancies about water in the lungs. Related to salinity. Horez said he didn't think there was much risk—the water Sanchez used for plumbing came out of the *marismas* in the first place. Sanchez said what about traces of lead and Horez replied that he was sure no examination would be looking for that. The lungs would be decomposed by the time they came to be examined, but there would still be evidence of drowning. That was all that any enquiry would want to know.

It was decided that they would both personally supervise the first part of the operation. A small tartan knee rug lying over the back of the leather sofa was used as an improvised hood. They held it on with a cord tied very tight round my neck. Before things went dark Horez was saying that the one thing that worried him was the fact that the villagers outside had seen me brought in, and Sanchez replied that once he gave the word, nothing was to be feared from them. I doubted this myself, but the point seemed of academic interest.

It was not, because when the police came over from Bonanza in river patrol boats, they learned at once that I had been taken inside Sanchez's great palace. They found us in the hall and there was a shoot out. Some of the cases containing birds got shattered and a stuffed lynx was filled with bullets once again. Concentrated on the moist little area of despair within the hood, I had hardly been aware of what was going on; only of the pain in my shoulder which the charcoal burner kept rattling with his heavy hand as he propelled me along. Then a bullet went through the calf of my leg and I crashed to the floor. When the hood was removed I saw a number of people lying around me. I saw dull black rifles and uniforms. Green and shining black, mackerel colours.

Mackerel numbers, too; when the *guardia civil* move it is either in twos or in twenties. I disagreed with Lorca's estimate that their brains were of lead and their souls patent leather. I thought Spanish policeman wonderful.

At daybreak I was taken across the river at last. From the patrol boat I looked back beyond the wide entrance of the Guadalquivir where the long golden line of Doñana with its ribbed hills of sand was visible, as bare and wild as it must have been when it greeted the Barbary pirates on their raids from Algiers and Tunis. Ahead was the refinement of San Lucar de Barremeda and Bonanza, whose townfolk seldom crossed to penetrate the wilderness. The two banks were linked by an occasional fishing boat or by a solitary heron flying over from the line of pine trees opposite.

Bonanza. A pleasant name. I remembered a village in Kildare similarly called Prosperous. I was brought to the great convent that dominated the town and put in charge of nuns. A policeman sat near keeping guard. The ward had a long window with vertical *rejas* through which I could see lines of ships tugging at their anchors, waiting for permission to go upriver to Seville. At night a lighthouse winked. Beneath the window I sometimes smelt frying fish or heard the roar of television from riverside bars. Twice I listened to rumbles and shouts from reporters demanding that I give a press conference.

I lay under a crucifix on a brass bed, one of whose legs was propped up with a piece of wood and a folded page from a magazine. From time to time a nun in brown would come in bearing an omelette or some fish cooked in milk or a couple of round continental aspirins that looked like peppermints or false pearls. Or a tract about Spanish missionary work abroad. It was not a long respite. After about ten days I had to give up perusing accounts of first communion services among slum dwellers in Lima.

I was taken to a prison in San Lucar. Smells and noises were familiar—half remembered from visits to Michael all those years ago. Countless interrogation sessions retraced once again my painful route around Doñana. I faced blasts of cold official anger. My behaviour had been criminally foolish. If I had given myself up promptly, as soon as I had come to Villafranco and heard about Patterson's death think of the lives that would have been saved. They brought down Joaquín to visit me, fresh from some mass demonstration of liberals and lawyers in Madrid. He recommended that I should see a psychiatrist, and didn't like it when I expressed amazement and told him Spanish psychiatry sounded like a contradiction in terms.

Corpses began to reappear. The man in the rice was found with difficulty. The factory management complained when work schedules had to be reorganized, and three days were wasted looking for him. He had moved a remarkable distance from where he fell. He was identified tentatively, and from photographs of identity documents I recognized the young man with the Moorish face whom I had first seen through my binoculars from the cork tree. An investigating team went to the *cano* to dig up Jaime. I was never quite certain if my theory was right, and if the bullet from the Austrian express rifle they found in his chest was the reason for the subsequent brisk court martial. Why, I wondered, had they waited for me with a rifle at the Lago de Dulce? Most of Sanchez's men whom I had encountered after I left Matalascanas had firearms. I asked one of my interrogators and he ceased his hectoring and bullying for a few minutes and became philosophical.

"Since the invention of gunpowder man has found it increasingly difficult to kill efficiently without the aid of firearms. How else could they stop you with certainty in the wastes of the marshes? Dulce's mud was close by to hide you."

"How did you know to cross the Guadalquivir to rescue me at Sanchez's place?"

"We had been watching Sanchez for some time. Two men died strangely the previous summer." It had not been easy to police the wild area—especially when there was nothing like proof that Sanchez did anything outside a spot of seasonal boar hunting. I was a criminal lunatic not to have gone straight to the barracks as soon as I got out of the marshes. However, it was Hubert's death—for which I was responsible—that made them suspicious. Horez had bungled it. The idea of implicating me was put out of gear by the timing. And Jaime had talked a little about Sanchez's trial experiment in pollution before he had died. And then I had been spotted on the banks of the Guadalquivir. An English sea captain had radioed the lighthouse people at San

Lucar. The police had drawn their own conclusions and moved in.

After poisoning Doñana, Don Sanchez would probably have sold the land. Possibly to Germans; they already had interest in the area at Matalascanas. It was also possible that he and Horez might have left Spain with as much money as they could lay hands on. They were extreme manifestations of the El Bunker mentality, believing firmly that their country had a limited future when revolution was once more on its way. The old order had changed too rapidly. They would be happier in some unpleasant dictatorship in South America—possibly Chile, where Horez had lived when he was doing his work on the effects of oil slicks on guano colonies.

The man whom I killed in the *choza* was never mentioned. No one claimed him or missed him. There is still time for his bones to be found.

In due course they dropped charges against me and let me go. My scientific image was battered, but not altogether crushed as I broke the egg of *aquila heliaca adalberti* they returned to me from Hubert's body. The rest of my collection I'll give away. Perhaps to the University of Seville if they want it. Not to Tring; they've got 250,000 eggs already. The BBC shelved the programme about Abel Chapman because of budget cutbacks. My agent is keen for me to publish a book describing exactly what happened on Doñana. The Spanish authorities won't be pleased, especially after my undertaking that I would do no such thing.

Hans and Irma made a little money out of the tape I gave them. The final agitation of digging up Jaime's body was too much for the imperial eagles, who abandoned their nest.

When I left Spain I went through Seville. It was the week of the Feria and the city was transformed by *casetas*, decorated arches and strings of lights. From early morning horses and carriages paraded, yellow-spoked wheels turning in the sand. Girls in long dresses were walking and riding with their sunburnt escorts.

A military band, whose sheets of music were clipped together with clothes-pegs, went by playing airs like "Las Islas Canary" or "Viva Navarra". I made my way to the Maria Louise park where the roses were in bloom. Shafts of light fell through the trees, even on the gloomy spot where Becquer's bust is guarded by two marble angels and three marble women. I read a few lines from his poems which are kept in a marble stoup beside him, and waited for Asunción.

She was in black and her mother was with her. Also her brother, wearing sunglasses under his big grey hat. The child was there too in a miniature frilled polka-dot dress that fell to her ankles. Her hair had been bleached so that it was bright gold and her nails were painted scarlet.

There were still marks on Asunción's face from the last beating she had received. But she seemed transformed with joy. Not at the sight of me nor of the three-foot teddy bear I had brought. Only now did she seem to realize how her husband's death had brought her release from a dreadful existence. She made no mention of the lies I had told her. Nor, with her family there, could we discuss any detail of our past encounter. What were her plans? She was joining her sister in Holland. It had not been easy getting visas and work permits, especially with the unemployment situation being the way it was, but her sister had managed to find her a job. The child would stay behind with her *abuela*. What was I going to do? Was I going away? We avoided any mention of Doñana. She smiled at me in a way that I remembered. I very much wanted to see her again.

I've written to her once or twice at an address in Arnhem.